"Could you use a little help, darlin'?"

Clay spoke softly in Niki's ear, but she still jumped as if he'd grabbed her. "I wish you'd quit sneaking up on me that way!"

She gave him an annoyed glance, but she still looked beautiful. A long wisp of hair blew across her mouth and she started to push it aside.

"Let me do that." Slowly he smoothed the silky lock back behind her ear. As his fingers skimmed the corner of her mouth, his body leapt to throbbing readiness in an instant.

"Oh, my," she said softly, breathlessly.

Clay let his hand fall aside, which required all of his considerable willpower. "You haven't answered my question."

"You asked a question?"

He laughed. "I asked if you needed any help."

"You don't want to do dishes." Her voice had recovered a bit of its usual spice.

"Says who?" He shoved up the sleeves of his shirt. "You'd be *astounded* at what I want to do."

Dear Reader,

And so with this book, the saga of the Keene triplets draws to a close...or does it?

I really hate to think about leaving Hard Knox, Texas. That's the biggest problem I have with miniseries: I never want to let go. I get to know and like the characters, not just my heroes and heroines but their friends and adversaries and relatives, the town where they hang out and the homes they live in. And no matter how happy the ending, there are always loose ends left behind, characters who deserve their own happily-ever-after.

But I wonder.... Niki, Toni and Dani may only *think* they're the last of the Keenes. I've heard rumors that their daddy, Wil Keene (the old reprobate), may have sown a few more wild oats than any of them know. It wouldn't surprise me a lick if a tenderfoot brother turned up one of these days to claim his share of the Bar K.

Another Keene GONE TO TEXAS? I may just have to look into that one of these days.

Thanks for joining me on this trip. I've had fun and hope you have, too.

Sincerely,

Ruth Jean Dale

THE COWGIRL'S MAN
Ruth Jean Dale

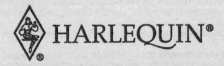

TORONTO • NEW YORK • LONDON
AMSTERDAM • PARIS • SYDNEY • HAMBURG
STOCKHOLM • ATHENS • TOKYO • MILAN • MADRID
PRAGUE • WARSAW • BUDAPEST • AUCKLAND

This book is dedicated to everyone who's ever wanted
to pull up stakes and start over.
Nothing ventured, nothing gained!

ISBN 0-373-25882-8

THE COWGIRL'S MAN

Copyright © 2000 by Betty Duran.

This edition published by arrangement with Harlequin Books S.A.

Visit us at www.eHarlequin.com

Printed in U.S.A.

1

NIKI KEENE attracted cowboys like honey attracted bees...like catnip attracted cats...like candy attracted kids. This natural phenomenon never failed to amaze Tilly Collins, proud grandmother to the Keene triplets, among whom Niki was the youngest by a mere twenty minutes.

Not that Tilly didn't think all three of her granddaughters were pretty special. Sitting at a wooden picnic table beneath a spreading pecan tree at the annual Hard Knox Fourth of July picnic and barbecue, she fanned herself idly while watching Niki turn aside her crowd of admirers with ease. As they said, practice makes perfect.

Back home in Elk Tooth, Montana, Niki had been labeled the "pretty one," Toni the "nice one" and Dani the "smart one." To their doting grandmother, each of the twenty-seven-year-old triplets was equally pretty, nice and smart. Still, she had to admit that there was a fortune to be made in bottling whatever it was that beautiful Niki had in such abundance.

It was only a passing thought, though, for like

everyone else who'd turned out at the city park for the celebration, Tilly was content just to enjoy the holiday atmosphere. With all the guests at the Keenes' Bar-K Dude Ranch present, she was free to simply enjoy herself like everybody else.

Crowds milled around, as Bar-K guests mingled with townsfolk and visitors to other Hill Country dude ranches. In the background, the amplified voice of Mayor Rosie Mitchell droned on. Mayor Rosie obviously enjoyed this part of the program, the presentation of awards and certificates and honors to what was beginning to feel like an interminable list of Hard Knoxers, as the local newspaper had long ago christened locals.

"Hi, Granny." Dani Keene Burke sat down on the picnic bench next to Tilly. "Whew, is it ever hot!"

Tilly glanced around for Dani's eleven-month-old daughter. "Not hot enough to make you forget what you did with Elsie, I hope."

Dani laughed and her brown eyes sparkled. Marriage to neighboring rancher Jack Burke had done wonders for her; Tilly had never seen Dani happier.

"Jack's got her," she said. "He'll be along as soon as he gets the kids a cup of lemonade."

Tilly nodded, knowing that "kids" in the plural included Jack's orphaned six-year-old nephew, Pete, adopted when Jack and Dani married. "Are Toni and Simon here yet?"

Dani nodded. "I saw the newlyweds drive up just

a few minutes ago. They'll be here soon." She glanced around at the crowd. "Where's Niki?"

Tilly pointed in the general direction. At that moment, the crowd parted and they saw Niki, still in the middle of a horde of male admirers. She was looking up with a non-committal smile at a tall cowboy.

She *was* gorgeous. Something about long black hair and blue eyes, Tilly supposed. Whatever it was, Niki had lots of it.

The loudspeaker sputtered and Tilly caught a single word from the mayor: *Niki.* Sure she'd misunderstood, Tilly glanced at Dani, who looked equally puzzled.

The mayor's voice became stronger: "Niki Keene, please, dear, will you come up here?"

Niki glanced toward her family, shapely black brows rising in a question. Dani shrugged and Toni, just arriving, waved.

"What do they want with Nik?" she inquired. "Simon and I just got here so—"

"Come on up, now," the mayor's amplified voice interrupted. "Don't be shy!"

At Mayor Rosie's urging, Niki's admirers lifted her to her feet and guided her toward the bandstand in the middle of the park. A sprinkling of applause built to a crescendo, despite the fact that no one appeared to know what was going on.

Tilly certainly didn't, but whatever it was, it was bound to be good. They didn't do bad things at community picnics in Hard Knox, Texas. So she smiled and applauded along with everybody else.

Mayor Rosie held up her arms for silence while Niki waited uneasily, casting her sometime boss dubious glances. Niki had gone to work as a barmaid at Rosie and Cleavon Mitchell's Sorry Bastard Saloon soon after the Keenes' move to Texas a few years back. She still worked there part-time, not because she needed the money anymore, but because she enjoyed it. Niki was a simple girl with simple needs.

"Friends and guests," Rosie said in her deep Texas drawl, "we got us a real nice surprise today. Seems like our own Niki Keene, darlin' of the Sorry Bastard, has been named a finalist in the Queen of the Cowgirls contest sponsored by Mother Hubbard's Wild West Duds! And I got a certificate here to prove it!" She waved the document triumphantly aloft.

Tilly frowned and muttered, "What's Mother Hubbard's Wild West Duds?"

Toni chuckled. "It's a western clothing company. In fact, it's a favorite of Niki's. That vest she's wearing is a Mother Hubbard." She glanced at Dani. "Can you believe it? Entering a contest and not even telling us, her own sisters."

"No, I *can't* believe it." Dani shook her head firmly. "There's something funny going on here. That contest has been publicized far and wide in magazines, even on TV. No *way* Niki would go for that. The winner will have to spend the next year being company spokesperson and posing for photographers. Niki would sooner walk on hot coals than do that."

Sad but true, Tilly thought as she watched a protesting Niki shake her head vehemently. If there was one thing her beautiful granddaughter didn't like it was being in the limelight.

Niki leaned forward to be heard via the microphone. "I'm afraid there's been a mistake, Rosie," she said, hastily amending that to, "Mayor Rosie."

Rosie grinned and shook her head, but her expression turned slightly desperate. "No mistake at all, Niki. That's your name on this certificate, see?"

"Nevertheless," Niki said in gentle but determined tones, "this is obviously some kind of a mistake. Thank you very much, but I didn't even enter the contest."

With a smile to soften her position, she turned away.

"Wait, Niki!" Now the mayor looked *really* worried. "This is no mistake, hon. Whether you entered or not, you've made the finals, which is a wonderful thing for your adopted hometown. Won't you—"

"I wish I could, but it's impossible. Thanks, but no thanks." With a wave of her hand, Niki walked down the steps and disappeared into the crowd.

A pregnant pause ensued. Then Granny sighed. "Niki doesn't even like horses," she announced, her voice clear in the stunned silence. "If those folks want a cowgirl, they've definitely got the wrong gal!"

LURKING NEARBY, Clay Russell, World Champion All-Around Cowboy and well-paid national spokesman for Mother Hubbard's Wild West Duds, heard every word the old lady said. Wearing subdued western garb and dark glasses, his hat pulled low over his eyes, he'd managed to avoid being recognized thus far. A desire to keep it that way was the only thing that prevented him from approaching the Mrs. Santa Claus look-alike.

Out of rodeo for the moment with an injury that had left him doubting his future, Clay was traveling from town to town and sometimes state to state at the insistence of Mother Hubbard herself—Eve Hubbard, autocratic guiding force behind the phenomenal success of the western clothing manufacturing company. His current assignment: to scope out the twelve finalists chosen from thousands of photographs generated by the contest and then report back to Eve.

Hard Knox was his final stop before heading back to Dallas to make his report. Eve not only wanted to know how each contestant looked in person, she wanted to know how Queen of the Cowgirls wannabes handled themselves when they were informed of their finalist status.

Niki Keene had failed that test, Clay thought, still

idly eavesdropping on her family, joined now by two men apparently married to her sisters. All the other finalists in all the other towns had squealed and jumped up and down and hugged—in some cases kissed—everyone in sight. This one had said a firm "thanks, but no thanks" and walked away.

Obviously, she wasn't Queen of the Cowgirls material—but she *was* drop-dead gorgeous. Although he'd only seen her for a few minutes, she'd formed an indelible impression in his mind's eye—heavy black hair hanging over her shoulders in thick braids to frame a perfectly oval face dominated by high cheekbones, full red lips and eyes so deep a blue they were almost purple. Her golden skin glowed and the curves of her body were as perfect as her face.

And if he wasn't mistaken, she was wearing Mother Hubbard's Wild West Duds: faded form-fitting jeans and a denim vest fastened across her breasts with leather tabs. The bottom edge of the vest barely met the waistband of her jeans, giving tantalizing glimpses of a taut middle. The shadowy cleft between her breasts, shown to advantage by the deep vee of the easy-fitting vest, made promises he suspected would easily be fulfilled.

So she was good-looking. So were all the others, he reminded himself. But judging by what the little old lady had just said about horses, Niki wasn't worthy of the title with all the perks and prizes that came with it. Too bad—but maybe there *had* been a mistake.

"How do you suppose this happened?" It was the sister bouncing the toddler on her lap who asked. "Niki was obviously dumfounded."

"Your guess is as good as mine, Dani." The other sister shrugged. "But she should go for it and grab it if she gets the chance. Tons of prizes come with that title. I know how Niki feels about exploiting her looks, but it's not like this would be the first time. She *was* Miss Elk Tooth who knows how many times, and Miss Texas Barmaid and Miss Sunshine for the weather people and Miss Smile for that dental association and Miss—"

"Oh, my!" The grandmother flung up her hands. "Don't go any further, Dani, for heaven's sake. She got finagled into each and every one of those titles."

Yeah, sure, Clay thought. *One title maybe, but all those? I don't think so.*

"*I* think she ought to do it."

"Now why would you say that, Jack?" The grandmother inquired mildly.

The man hovering over the sister with the baby, the one who looked like a rancher, shrugged. "It'd be good for the town. We could put it in the Bar-K brochure and it would be good for business."

"You talk like she's already won," the other man remarked.

Both sisters blinked in surprise and the one with the baby said, "And your point is what, Simon?"

The man Simon, who *didn't* look like a rancher, a cowboy or any other country type, leaned down and kissed the top of Toni's head. "Just because Niki's great looking doesn't mean this contest is a slam dunk. She isn't the most beautiful girl in the world, after all. Toni is."

"Simon!" Toni gave him a satisfied glance. "You're prejudiced."

"Newlyweds are supposed to be prejudiced," Grandma said. "Dani, what do you think? Would Niki take it?"

"Absolutely not." Dani, still bouncing the baby on her knee, shook her head vehemently. "After what happened the last time, she swore her Miss Whoever career was over."

"What happened?" Simon inquired.

"The contest coordinator got fresh with her," Dani said darkly. "They also over-scheduled her and were downright unreasonable in their demands. So no, I don't think she'll change her mind and I don't suppose I can really blame her."

Clay edged away. It was just about time for him to hit the road for Dallas to report on the total unsuitability of this particular contestant. Regardless of what her family might think, she wouldn't be a shoo-in even if she competed.

"And then..." The grandmother sighed. "There's that thing she has about *horses*."

A quick glance showed Clay nothing but uniformly glum faces. What the hell was this about Niki Keene and horses, he wondered. Not that it mattered. She had too many other negatives and only one positive that he could see.

Grandmother turned suddenly brisk. "It's not up to us anyway. Dani, I'm going back to the ranch now. If you and Jack would like to stay and help Toni and Simon herd our dudes, I'll take the children with me."

"Jack?" Dani deferred to her husband.

"Sounds good. We can drop by the Sorry Bastard and try to talk some sense into our stubborn beauty queen."

"'Try' is the word, all right." She turned to the other couple. "Okay with you guys?"

While they made their plans, Clay drifted away. He really ought to hit the road for Dallas. It was going to be late before he got there as it was.

Still—

What was Niki Keene doing at a saloon? He'd noticed the Sorry Bastard on his arrival in town hours earlier. Was she a closet drinker or did she work there? Unbidden, her image flashed again across his mind's eye and he shook it off. No way she could be as good-looking as he remembered.

Nevertheless, he might just trail along to the Sorry

Bastard out of simple curiosity—and to take one more look.

WHEN NIKI SAW her sisters walk through the door to the Sorry Bastard, she was ready for them. They'd be on her case, no doubt about it. They'd nagged her into accepting the Miss Elk Tooth title back in Montana, even though she'd never entered the contest; they'd nagged her into taking the Miss Texas Barmaid title and the Cowboys' Dream Girl title and all the rest.

But Queen of the Cowgirls? That was going much too far. What about truth in advertising?

Niki turned toward the bar, stifling a smile. She wasn't a cowgirl, had never been a cowgirl, didn't want to be a cowgirl. The fact that her family owned a dude ranch hadn't changed her mind about that one iota. Let them saddle the horses and guide the trail rides and herd the cows. Niki was perfectly content cleaning cabins and peeling potatoes.

"Two draft beers, Ken," she said to the mustachioed bartender. While she waited, she surveyed the room with detached interest. The large barroom with its hardwood floors and broad log pillars boasted a good-size crowd, many of them strangers in town for just a day or two for the annual festivities. Then there were always the dudes, who came and went so regularly that—

Her restless gaze stopped short on the broad back

of a man standing before that god-awful display Rosie and Cleavon had made of Niki's past exploits. It was an utter embarrassment to her that her pictures took up the entire back wall: Niki as beauty queen with satin ribbons across her chest and insincere smiles on her lips. They said it was good for business and maybe it was, but she felt funny about it just the same.

But who was the man lingering before the display? A stranger, she knew instantly, without even seeing his face. Not a dude, judging by the way he wore his jeans and western shirt, and the way he'd removed his hat and held it in front of him as he perused the wall with care.

Slim hipped and broad shouldered, long legged and narrow waisted... As she watched, he moved slightly and a beam of light from the dusty window touched his hair, turning it from dark to golden-brown. Thick hair, worn stylishly shaggy—

"Beers are ready, Nik."

Ken's voice snapped her out of her examination of the stranger and, gratefully, she turned. She didn't like to be distracted that way. She wouldn't say she was exactly down on men, but she wasn't exactly "up" on them, either.

She delivered the beer, then bowed to the inevitable and made her way to her sisters' table. They gave her such ingratiating grins that she knew she was in for it.

"Where's the rest of the family?" she inquired, trying to head them off at the pass.

"Granny took the kids home and the men are rounding up dudes," Dani said. "Toni and I thought we'd drop by and say hello to the next Queen of the Cowgirls." Her brown eyes sparkled with amusement.

"Ha-ha, very funny." Niki dredged up a resentful smile. Suddenly she straightened beneath the impact of a new thought. "Did you two enter me in that contest?" It was more accusation than question. "Because if you did, I swear I'll—"

"Not me!" Dani threw up her hands and looked at Toni.

"Not me, either, although obviously somebody did. But now that it's happened..." She fixed Niki with an assessing stare. "You might have been a bit hasty, Nik. This is a biggie."

"Oh, *really!*"

"Don't scoff, this contest is national. The winner gets a modeling contract and a year's worth of public appearances for that clothing company. What's the name...?"

"Mother Hubbard." Niki looked down at herself. "As luck would have it, I wear a lot of clothes from that label."

"It's fate," Toni declared. "The winner also gets a great Mother Hubbard wardrobe."

Niki groaned. "Like I care? I can afford to buy my

own clothes. Look, we're really busy around here. Can I get you something or did you just drop by to torment me?"

"I'll have a diet anything," Dani said.

"Me, too," Toni agreed. "But seriously, Niki, you should think this over more carefully. If you were Queen of the Cowgirls, it'd be great for the town, and the ranch, too."

Niki didn't know whether to laugh or cry at that comment. "Antoinette Keene, you bite your tongue! I'm not even a cowgirl, let alone *queen*. They could get me for fraud."

"Don't be silly." Dani waved a hand airily. "It's just a name. They don't care if you're really a cowgirl, they just care if you look good in their clothes. And you do, so what's the problem?"

"The problem, Sister dear, is that I'd feel like a fraud whether anyone else thought so or not. Plus I don't want to be a model—" She shuddered. "—and I sure don't want to get tied up for an entire year."

"But the town! The ranch!"

"Are doing very well, thank you very much." Niki glanced around restlessly. "Look, I'm perfectly happy with my life as it is. I don't need any new complications."

"Maybe you won't win," Toni suggested hopefully. "I mean, silly as that seems, there are eleven other finalists according to what I read in some magazine or other. The winner will be chosen in Dallas, I think it is. So you could just take the publicity for being a finalist—for the good of the town, of course—and hope you'd lose."

Nikki shivered. "Do you have any idea how much I would detest standing up with eleven other contestants to be judged like a Holstein cow? If I was ever in doubt—and I wasn't!—you just made the decision for me, Toni. No, no, a thousand times no. End of conversation."

"But—"

"*Hey, Niki!*"

Niki turned toward the voice automatically, then grimaced. "Oh, good lord, there's the reporter from the *Hard Knox Hard Times*. Don't tell me she wants to talk about this cowgirl nonsense!"

"Then I won't tell you," Dani said smugly, "but it's a big deal, whether you want to admit it or not."

"I'm too busy." With a quick wave toward the reporter, Niki shrugged as if she had no choice, then turned toward the bar. "I'll get those sodas right away."

"Coward!" Toni called after her fleeing sister.

Niki ignored that unjust comment.

THE SALOON was so dim that with his dark glasses firmly in place, Clay could barely see to make his way across the room between crowded tables and thick log supports. He'd spotted an empty table behind one of the broad beams near where the Keene sisters sat. If he could just reach it before someone else spotted it—

Stepping around the log barrier, he came face-to-face with a cowboy who looked equally startled.

"Sorry," Clay said, "but I'm after that—"

Table. The one at which the young cowboy now sat, smiling up ingenuously.

"No problem," the cowboy said. He stuck out his hand. "Name's Dylan Sawyer. You lookin' for a place to sit?"

No, Clay was tempted to snap back, *I just enjoy dashing across crowded rooms.* Instead he said, "Yeah, and I almost had one." He shook the other man's hand. "Call me Clay."

Dylan Sawyer nodded. "Will do. I'm expectin' a few friends, but you're welcome to join us." He indicated an empty chair.

Clay didn't have to be asked twice. Sitting down, he put his hat, brim up, on the table. "You work around here?" he inquired.

Dylan nodded. "At the Bar-K."

Clay's scalp prickled. "I...think I've heard of it."

"Belongs to the Keene triplets. You a stranger?"

"Just passing through."

"You still might'a seen Niki Keene earlier when they tried to give her that Cowgirl prize, whatever it was."

"Queen of the Cowgirls. Yeah, I saw. But...I thought she was just a finalist."

Dylan laughed incredulously. "Same difference. I figure it's in the bag. That is, if anybody can get her to change her mind about pullin' out of the contest."

Civic pride accounted for the young cowboy's confidence, Clay figured. Curiosity made him add, "Think she'll go for it?"

"Who knows." Dylan shrugged. "But if she does, she'll win and I'd put money on that. I mean, did you ever see a better-lookin' woman in your entire life?" Twisting around in his chair, he stared pointedly at the bar where Niki was picking up another tray of drinks. "She's real nice, too."

"She's a looker, all right," Clay conceded softly.

And just at that very moment she looked up and her gaze locked with his.

THE STRANGER'S bold stare shot through Niki like a jolt of electricity and she caught her breath. It was the man she'd seen before, only she'd seen him from the back. He'd been looking at her pictures and now he was looking at *her* with an intensity that made her pulse pound. Questions arose.

Why in the world was a cowboy wearing dark glasses in a dim bar?

And why was he sitting at a table with Dylan Sawyer as if they were old friends?

"Niki, table nine's waitin' for those drinks."

"Sorry, Ken." Flustered, she picked up the tray and tried to ignore the stranger. She was sure she couldn't actually feel his gaze pinned between her shoulder blades but it certainly seemed as if she could. Every hair on her head prickled with awareness.

And she was going to have to walk up to that table and take his order. Sure, she could get Tracy to do it but that would be cowardly. Niki was no coward.

Beers delivered, she straightened her shoulders and pasted a smile on her lips. For a moment she was tempted to find that reporter and subject herself to the unavoidable newspaper interview, but that would only delay the inevitable.

Chin up, she approached the two men. The closer she got, the better the stranger looked—except she couldn't see his eyes. She could see the hard jaw that contrasted so strikingly with a full and sexy mouth, though. When he smiled his teeth were an even white flash against dark skin.

"Dylan." She acknowledged the young rider for the Bar-K with a dip of her head. Her gaze swept over to include his companion. "You gentlemen ready to name your poison?"

"I'll have a draft," Dylan said. "Clay?"

For a moment the stranger named Clay hesitated. Then he rose slowly, strong hands braced on the tabletop and sunglass-shaded gaze boring holes in her. "I guess there's nothing here I really want," he said, softly and politely. Picking up his hat, he nodded, turned and walked out of the saloon.

Niki stared after him, lips parted in astonishment. She couldn't believe what had just happened.

The man hadn't been talking about a drink at all. He'd had something entirely different on his mind and she didn't think she liked the possibilities that presented.

"Beer coming up," she snapped at Dylan, as if it were his fault. And for the rest of the day she brooded about the good-looking stranger who might have been putting her down...or maybe not.

2

CLAY CLIMBED INTO his dusty black pickup truck and drove out of Hard Knox, Texas, in a blue funk. Hell, no wonder Niki Keene declined to compete. She didn't have to. Her friends and family would do it for her.

Thinking dark thoughts, he headed east. Eventually he'd hit Highway 35 and then it was a straight shot north to Dallas. It wouldn't take him more than five, six hours at the most.

That was five or six hours to brood over the delectable but elusive Niki Keene. Jeez!

By the time she'd reached his table at the Sorry Bastard, he'd been tight as a drum and jumpy as a mustang with a burr under its saddle. The way people in that town talked, she was some kind of goddess or something. That didn't sit too well with Clay since he was the one accustomed to such adulation, not the other way around.

Of course, in all fairness he had to remind himself that none of that came from her. Her only crime appeared to be a reluctance to be judged...how had she put it? Like a Holstein cow.

That brought a reluctant grin. So, she had a sense of humor. Big deal.

She also had a whole pack of other titles judging from what he'd seen on the back wall of the Sorry Bastard. She'd been named every Miss-Whoever-That-Came-Down-The-Pike. She was on a roll, gathering in every beauty title around. So what was Queen of the Cowgirls, chopped liver?

Brooding mile after mile, he hit the highway just north of Austin and turned north. By then he'd just about convinced himself that:

One, Niki Keene wasn't as good-looking as he'd at first thought.

Two, if she didn't want to compete for the title, he, for one, wouldn't try to force it on her.

And three, she must not be too bright because if she had the sense God gave a goose, she'd see what a great opportunity this was.

But damn! She'd been wearing Mother Hubbard's Wild West Duds and she filled them out *real* good.

CLAY SLEPT late the next morning in the small but luxurious apartment Mother Hubbard herself had provided for a home base while he ran her errands. Although he rarely used it and considered his uncle's spread in Oklahoma an uneasy home, it had turned out to be a handy *pied-a-terre,* as Mother called it.

"Ped-a-*what?*" Clay had demanded incredulously.

"Home away from home, dear boy," she'd explained with a somewhat superior smile. *"C'est la vie!"*

That was Mother Hubbard.

He took his time over breakfast at a handy diner before heading for the head office of Mother Hubbard's Wild West Duds. He'd come to know the towering steel-and-glass structure since he'd been hired as company spokesman just over two years ago.

At first he'd felt ridiculous, getting all duded up and having his picture taken with all the solemnity of an Important Happening. After a while he got used to it, though, and now it was just another job—a job that brought in big bucks.

"Mr. Russell!" The receptionist beamed at him. "Welcome back."

"Thanks, Marla. The boss lady in town?" He rolled his eyes toward the elevators that rose to the top floor where Mother Hubbard held court.

Marla's smile revealed perfect teeth. "Not only that—she's expecting you."

"She doesn't even know I'm in town," he objected, startled by her comment.

She shrugged, eyes widening. "Don't ask me, I just work here. But I've heard it said she has eyes in the back of her head." Smiling, she returned her attention to her computer screen.

Clay crossed the lobby toward the elevator, his boot heels clicking on the marble. Mother always seemed to know everything so why was he surprised? Punching the up-button, he waited patiently, his gaze wandering around the lobby, sensing a change.

Something new had been added: a blowup of a famous old ad campaign that had sold a helluva lot of denim. It featured "Mother Hubbard," a lovely white-haired little old lady who—now that he noticed—looked a lot like Niki Keene's grandma. She looked straight into the camera, pointing her finger and wearing a mischievous smile while declaring, "You should listen to your mother!"

Yeah, he thought as he stepped into the elevator. Listening to Mother Hubbard was what had gotten him into this strange world in the first place—that and a ton of money.

THE REAL Mother Hubbard looked absolutely nothing like "Mother Hubbard," a fact that never failed to startle Clay. The first time he'd met the sleek, blond and sophisticated Eve Hubbard he'd thought it was a joke.

It wasn't. Eve herself had explained why she'd hired an actress to play the part of Mother Hubbard in public—because Eve herself was *not* the image she wanted for her company. When the actress died three years ago, Clay had been brought in as spokesman to "take the company in a new direction."

"I design the clothes because I love them, but I can't wear them and I sure as hell can't represent them properly in public," Eve had explained bluntly, her scarlet mouth curving down in an unhappy line. "I just don't project the proper image, hence the Queen of the Cowgirls contest."

She'd winked. "Every cowboy needs a queen," she'd said. "I'm doing this for you, dear."

"Oh, yeah."

"You're only half the package, darling. When I launched this company twenty years ago on a damned shoestring, I vowed never to let vanity, mine or anybody else's, get between me and a strong bottom line."

She obviously never had. Today her company was a multi-million-dollar success with Eve still flying high as chief designer and eccentric head honcho. Aggressive and smart, she terrorized most of the people she dealt with.

Clay liked her.

Her secretary waved him through with a smile and he entered the plush and modern office—another shock considering that the company produced down-home western styles. Eve rose quickly from behind a massive glass-and-chrome desk, her sleek red suit the only touch of color in the room.

"Darling!" Coming around the desk, she offered her porcelain cheek for his kiss.

"Howdy, Mother." He pressed his lips to her cool skin.

"Do tell me about your adventures." She plucked

a manila folder off the desk before drawing him toward a black leather couch near the glass wall.

"Saw a lot of good-lookin' women." He sat down beside her.

"Twelve of them?" Eve asked sharply, spilling out the contents of the folder on the cocktail table: the eight-by-ten glossy photographs which had earned these women entrance into the finalists' round. "Any duds, pardon the expression, in the bunch?"

Clay laughed. "Not a one. They're all real good-lookers."

"How about the girl from Tulsa?" She slid a photo from the messy pile before her and held it up.

"Pretty, but she's kinda...guess you'd call it inarticulate. Put a microphone in her face and she starts to giggle."

"She's out, then."

Startled, Clay frowned, thinking that the rest of the contest judges might not agree with her.

"How about that one near Denver?" She held up another photo, this one of a dazzling green-eyed blonde.

"A possibility. She looks good but there's something kinda...I guess you'd say cold about her. Her personality, I mean."

"I wonder if that would photograph," Eve mused, squinting at the color likeness. She sighed and tossed it aside. "Let me think.... There's got to be one in this group who's just right." She brightened. "How

about the girl in that little jerkwater town south of
here...Hard Hat, Hard Work—something like that."

"Hard Knox."

"That's it." Eve pulled out a photograph of Niki
wearing a big grin and a Stetson. "How was she?"

How was she? Clay stared at the picture, startled
all over again by the brilliance of those dark blue
eyes, the vitality of the straight black hair. He'd spent
most of the night trying to figure her out and failed
miserably.

"She's...a good possibility," he said carefully, surprised to find he wasn't ready to explain Niki's reluctance to participate just yet.

"And the girl in Cheyenne..."

Eve continued questioning Clay closely and he answered as fully as he could, considering the fact that
most of the things she wanted to know weren't really
things he noticed—carriage, grace, presence. If that's
what Eve wanted, she should have sent someone
else.

The only contestant he'd noticed who *had* all those
things to any discernable degree was Niki Keene and
she didn't want any part of the Queen of the Cowgirls competition. He really should tell Eve and get it
over with but she was going to ask a bunch of questions he wasn't prepared to answer so to hell with it.

"How many were wearing my clothes?" she asked
suddenly, her expression moving from inquiring to
serious.

He was ready for that question but sorry it had come so early in the proceedings. "Only one that I'm sure of," he said slowly. "Niki Keene was wearing Mother Hubbard's Wild West Duds but—"

"Niki Keene...this pretty thing?" She waved the picture.

"Yes, but—"

"Can she talk beyond monosyllables?"

"Yes, but—"

"Is she as attractive in person?"

"More so."

"Guess that settles it, then."

"Settles what?"

"The winner of the first Queen of the Cowgirls title. That's what we've been talking about, right?"

"Sure, but—"

"What's your problem, darling?" she snapped. "Aren't you used to women who can make decisions?" To emphasize her point, she snapped her scarlet-tipped fingers.

"I thought this was an honest contest," he blurted.

"It is."

"How can it be if you just decide who the winner is on a whim?"

"Good grief, the boy's disillusioned!" Smiling almost diabolically, she patted his knee. "Don't be. I always go with my gut instincts which is what makes me great." She raised one carefully groomed brow.

"Besides, I'm the final judge so what difference does it make if I pick the winner now or later?"

"I'd guess it makes a lot of difference to the other contestants."

"Don't get huffy, dear boy. *They* won't know. It'll be our little secret, if that makes you feel any better."

"It doesn't," he said bluntly. "Before this goes any further, there's something I think you need to know."

She straightened and her hazel eyes narrowed fractionally. "Such as?"

"Niki Keene has shown a certain...reluctance to compete."

"What the hell does 'a certain reluctance' mean?"

"That when the mayor made the announcement and presented the certificate, she said thanks but no thanks—and that's a direct quote."

Eve's shock was almost comical. "You're kidding!"

"I wish."

"But...what woman in her right mind would turn down this kind of opportunity? Women have committed murder for less!"

"That's what her friends and family were asking. She just kept saying she wasn't interested."

"Hmmm..." She rose to stalk to the desk and back again. Stopping, she fixed him with a determined gaze. "Did she mean it?"

"Sounded like it to me."

"Hmm... You say she's as gorgeous in person as she is in that picture?"

"Gorgeous-er, even."

"And she was wearing Mother Hubbard's Wild West Duds."

"That's right." And she looked damn good in them. "But if she doesn't want to compete, nobody can force her," he pointed out.

"Who's talking force?" Eve's head lifted and she grinned suddenly, as if she'd just puzzled out the problem to her satisfaction. "I'm more subtle than that, darling."

"You could'a fooled me," he observed dryly. "How do you intend to pull off this miracle of persuasion?"

"Not me, love. You. *You're* going to convince our reluctant heroine that she longs for the Queen of the Cowgirls title more than anything in her entire little world."

"No way!" He stared at her, appalled. "How am I, a perfect stranger, supposed to—"

"That's the key, because you *are* perfect, stranger or otherwise. Why do you think I signed you on as Mother's spokesman? Because you support charitable causes and are kind to kids and animals?"

"How do you know I'm kind to—?"

"I have ways of finding these things out." She waved off his astonishment. "With your looks and charm, she won't stand a chance."

"Gimme a break." Embarrassed, he sunk lower into the butter-soft leather. "I can't just—"

"You certainly can. I want you to hightail it back to Hard Times—"

"Hard Knox."

"—and convince this girl that she must compete." She marched to her desk and sat down, began pulling open drawers in search of something, adding, "Without telling her the contest is basically fixed, of course."

Clay gritted his teeth. This was not shaping up to his liking. "No," he said. "I won't do it."

She pulled a sheaf of papers from a drawer with an exclamation of satisfaction, slammed the drawer closed again and leaned back in her massive leather chair. "Of course you'll do it."

Her certainty sent up red flags. "I said I wouldn't."

"But you're going to change your mind as soon as I point out a certain little paragraph in your contract." She tossed the sheaf of papers on the desktop. "It's the one that says I can terminate your services on a moment's notice if you refuse any reasonable assignment that doesn't conflict with your primary career which is rodeo, and which of course, this doesn't."

He surged to his feet. "Dammit, Eve, I—"

"Darling, darling, don't despair!" She came to meet him, all motherly concern. "I'm not asking you to do anything immoral or illegal. I'm simply sending you to convince this beautiful child that Mother Hubbard can make her life infinitely better."

"While selling a whole passel of jeans and tight shirts."

"That, too," she said with a satisfied smile. "Look, I wouldn't pressure you this way—"

"Yeah, right." He rolled his eyes, feeling somewhat mollified.

"—but I have such a strong feeling that this is right for everyone concerned. You know about my 'feelings,' of course."

He nodded, because everyone at M.H.W.W.D. knew. She always based business decisions on those "feelings." This made the suits crazy and delighted everyone else, including Clay up to but not including the present moment.

She patted his cheek. "If you pull this off, and I'm confident you will, there'll be a nice fat bonus in it for you," she wheedled. "Don't be difficult, darling. Trust me. This will work. Not only that—it should be a lot of fun, hanging around some little burg where you'll be a big hero, spending time with a drop-dead gorgeous woman. What part of 'summer fun' don't you understand?"

Clay sighed, because she had a point. He was not adverse to getting to know Niki Keene better...a lot better, he realized as his groin tightened. "Give me time to think about this," he hedged, unwilling to concede total victory so quickly. "Maybe I have plans. Maybe I—"

"Love to," she cut him off, "but we've got a press conference slated in a few hours to announce details of the actual contest. It'll be held at my ranch—had I told you that?"

"No." He knew her "ranch" was actually a spectacular estate on the outskirts of Dallas where her minions raised a few head of longhorns and a few quarter horses often used as publicity props for her company. It would provide an elegant setting for a dozen beautiful girls.

She nodded. "Well, it is. Now, I've just got time to brief you and then we've got to doll you up in the new Duds line. Trust me, Clay, this is going to be a great boost for everyone involved...."

NIKI BALANCED the tray of dirty dishes on one shoulder with professional ease and smiled at the handsome mustached man sitting alone at a table at the Sorry Bastard. "Hi, Travis. What brings you to town on a Tuesday?"

Travis Burke, Dani's father-in-law and a popular rancher whose XOX Ranch was one of the biggest dude-and-working outfits in the country, grinned back at her. It was certainly easy to see where his son, Jack, got his good looks.

"Pa's got a doctor's appointment," Travis said, referring to the elderly but still plenty salty Austin

Burke. "Doc Wilson's got an emergency so who knows when he'll be done?" He shrugged. "I figured I'd grab a bite and then take something back to Pa. He's convinced he'll lose his place in line if he leaves."

"He could be right. What can I get you?"

"A hamburger and a beer should do it."

"Comin' right up."

When she returned a few minutes later with his order, he nodded toward an empty chair. "I sure do hate to eat alone," he said plaintively. "Since most of the rush seems to be over, maybe you could sit down a minute or two?"

He was right; only two other tables were being used and the occupants of both were finishing their food. "Don't mind if I do," she said, sitting.

He piled condiments on his burger: pickles and onion and lettuce and tomato. "I've been wantin' to ask if you ever found out who entered you in that contest," he remarked.

She sighed. "It was Mason Kilgore, a photographer I worked for in Montana before we came here. He used to take pictures of me when he was bored. He got the bright idea to send one in and pulled it out of his files."

Travis picked up his burger carefully. "It *was* a bright idea, apparently. When's the contest?"

She looked at him in surprise. "I don't know. Since I don't intend to participate, it really doesn't matter."

"You meant what you said the Fourth of July, huh?" He took a big bite of his burger, his gaze curious.

"Of course, I did," she said indignantly. "Why on earth would I want to—"

"*Niki!*"

Dylan rushed across the room, the sharp urgency in his voice making her start. Whatever had him in an uproar was all to the good, though, since she'd been meaning to track him down for some straight talk ever since she'd seen him with that strange, and very attractive, cowboy on the Fourth of July.

He galloped up, his face actually pale beneath his wide-brimmed hat. She felt a rush of alarm.

"What is it, Dylan? You look like you've seen a ghost."

"I practically did." He tossed a newspaper onto the table, half-covering Travis's plate. "Have y'all seen that?"

"Today's *San Antonio Sun?* No."

"Then take a look," he almost yelled, stabbing his forefinger at the page. "I wouldn't believe it if I hadn't read it in the paper." He shook his head in disbelief.

Heart in her throat, Niki leaned over the page and saw a photograph—a photograph of the cowboy she'd just been thinking about. Helplessly she looked up at Dylan, who nodded.

"Yep, that's him—none other than Clay Russell,

World Champion Cowboy, in the flesh. And fool that I was, I set right over there—" He pointed dramatically at a table. "—and talked to him and never had any the least idea who he was."

"His name's Clay Russell?" She was having trouble grasping this. Leaning over, she read the caption.

Clay Russell, official spokesman for Mother Hubbard's Wild West Duds, was announcing details of the contest to crown the first Queen of the Cowgirls. There, among the list of finalists, her own name leaped out at her.

Incensed, she looked up to find both men staring at her. "How dare he do this!" she exclaimed. "My name's still there and he knows I have no intention of taking part in that stupid contest. What part of 'no thanks' doesn't he understand?"

Dylan frowned. "You really meant what you said about turning it down?"

"Why on earth would I say it if I didn't mean it?"

The cowboy shrugged. "I dunno. I thought..." He darted a guarded glance at Travis, placidly munching while watching the goings-on with interest. "I thought you just wanted to be coaxed."

Niki groaned. "Dylan Sawyer, you know me better than that."

"Well, heck, Niki, a woman can always change her mind." He shuffled his feet awkwardly. "Now that you know Clay Russell's involved..."

"That doesn't change a darn thing."

"I dunno, Niki." Travis wiped his fingers on a paper napkin, his expression dubious. "This could be an awful good thing for the town, having you sashaying around the country as Miss Queen of the Cowgirls or whatever it is."

"*Et tu*, Travis?" She gave him a reproachful look.

"Now, think about it," he urged. "From what I hear, you'll get money, prizes, fame, glamour...."

"I don't *want* any of that."

Dylan leaned forward. "You'll get your picture took with Clay Russell," he said. "That wouldn't be none too shabby."

Niki shivered. She didn't want her picture taken with the handsome stranger who'd confused and unnerved her. Remembering his final words in light of this new information—*I don't think there's anything here I really want*—made her suppose *he* thought she wouldn't have a chance of winning anyway.

Which should make her feel better but didn't. She picked up her tray. "I don't want to talk about this," she said. "I appreciate your good intentions but the subject isn't open for discussion."

"But Niki—"

Undeterred, she went about her business, which lasted until the next customer entered.

"Have you seen the *San Antonio Sun*?"

That's all she heard for the rest of her shift. By the time she turned in her apron and prepared to leave, she was heartily sick of all the gratuitous advice she'd been receiving, all of it the same: do it for *us*. Do it for the *town*.

Well, she wouldn't! Not this time. She'd—

"Hey, Niki!"

She whirled to find Miguel Reyes, a cowboy she'd known ever since she moved to Texas, standing there grinning at her. She grinned back, but warily, waiting for him to ask if she'd seen that darned newspaper.

Too bad, really. Miguel was one good-looking guy, and just as nice as he was cute. She'd actually been thinking lately that she might want to go out with him.... She wasn't too crazy about cowboys as a rule but her choices were limited and she did sometimes get lonely for a little male companionship.

"Got a minute?" he asked, twisting his hat between big, competent hands.

"Yes." Niki said cautiously. Now he'd ask her if she knew who the stranger at the picnic had been and she'd have to go through the whole song-and-dance again.

"Uh...would you like to go to the movies with me Friday night?"

"Miguel, I've been all through this and—" She stopped short. "What did you say?"

"I asked you to go to the movies with me Friday. Any chance?"

"There's always a chance," she said lightly, trying

to catch her balance again. "But Friday...that's not good for me."

"Why not?" Miguel asked softly. "Got to wash your hair or something?"

Niki felt hot blood rush into her cheeks. "No, of course not," she protested, but he'd hit the nail right on the head. "I...uh...have to help with the dude talent night at home. I'm sorry..."

And she really *was*, sorry she hadn't yelled "Yes!" at the top of her lungs. Now it was too late.

Watching Miguel make his way through the barroom, she sighed. If she didn't quit turning down men who wanted to date her, they'd eventually quit asking.

Or maybe not. She didn't view many of them as favorably as she did Miguel and some of them had come back so many times she'd lost count.

Unbidden, a mental picture of the stranger—Clay Russell, she knew his name now—flashed before her eyes. He didn't look as if he'd ask anyone for anything.

He probably didn't have to, she thought darkly. He was probably fighting the girls off with a stick.

Not *this* girl; never this girl.

3

IT TOOK CLAY more than two weeks to make it back to Hard Knox because he and Eve agreed that it wouldn't be a good idea to let Niki Keene know they were out to get her, so to speak. To cover their tracks, Eve arranged a tour for her star asset: stops at all the other eleven finalists' hometowns for meetings with the contestants, photos to see how they looked with Clay, and interviews to make sure they could "talk."

She reasoned that if they created a big enough public hullabaloo, Niki would feel obligated to cooperate even before they got there.

Hell, Clay thought philosophically, it was worth a shot.

As a result, he hit Hard Knox on a Saturday afternoon in late July, this time amidst much fanfare and ballyhoo. A reception committee met him at the edge of town and led him to the park where he'd skulked on the Fourth of July. There the mayor waited. Almost before Clay could climb out of his pickup truck, the park began to fill with curious and eager citizens of all ages.

Escorted to the bandstand by the rotund chief of

police, he was met by the beaming mayor. Behind her, a couple of photographers hovered, fingering the cameras draped around their necks. One would be in Eve's hire and the other was doubtless from the local newspaper.

The mayor nodded happily. "Rosie Mitchell," she said, grabbing his hand and shaking it with both of hers. "Welcome to our fair city, Mr. Russell."

"Call me Clay." He looked around for Niki and spotted her sisters almost at once but the reluctant contestant herself was not in evidence. "Uhh...I don't seem to see—"

"That'll wait." Rosie hauled him to the edge of the platform and held up her hands for attention. "Folks, I'd like y'all to meet Clay Russell, World Champion All-Around Cowboy. Let's give him a big ol' Hard Knox welcome!"

At her urging, everyone applauded, some politely but most with enthusiasm. Clay acknowledged their welcome with a smile and a friendly wave but his thoughts were elsewhere, with a certain blue-eyed black-haired malcontent.

When the applause died away, he tried again. "Mayor Mitchell, I don't see our contestant anywhere. I hope Ms. Keene—"

"Yes, yes, we'll talk about that," Rosie said. "But first—"

One of the men loitering nearby rushed forward, carrying a large gilt key.

"The key to the city," Rosie said expansively, offering it to Clay with a flourish. "We're mighty proud to welcome you to Hard Knox and hope you'll stay around long enough to appreciate lots of good old-fashioned Texas hospitality."

Somewhat taken aback, Clay accepted the key to the accompaniment of more applause. About eighteen inches long and made of balsa wood, it glittered with brilliant metallic gold paint. A bright blue ribbon streamed from the shaft.

"I'm overwhelmed," he said. "Thank you all for this nice welcome. Now if I can just meet our contestant—"

"You can meet everyone!" Rosie waved expansively to the crowd. She added in a joking tone, "Now don't y'all push and shove, folks." She gave him a conspiratorial wink. "I'm sure you'll all get to shake the hand of our honored guest—maybe even get yourself an autograph."

And that's what happened for the next hour and forty-five minutes. Not once did Niki Keene show her beautiful face, nor did her sisters join the line of autograph seekers. In fact, after a while they wandered off.

This did not portend well for the success of his mission but he wouldn't let *that* little quibble get him down. It was in his own best interest to get Nikki to compete, so compete she would.

OVER AT the nearly empty Sorry Bastard Saloon, Niki strove in vain to ignore what she knew was going on outside. She wanted nothing to do with the duplicitous Mr. Russell but neither did she want to be rude. Maybe if she simply stayed away, he'd take the hint.

But she couldn't forget the words he'd said on the Fourth of July: *nothing I want here.*

Definitely an insult.

Cleavon, working behind the bar, waved her over. Rosie was definitely the more popular member of that duo but Niki had always been fond of her *other* boss, too.

Tall and thin, he'd wrapped the white bar apron around his skinny body a couple of times. As always, his long brown hair was pulled back into a wispy ponytail that drooped at the nape of his neck.

Flopping a towel on the bar, he leaned forward. "Why don'cha just go on over to th' park?" he urged plaintively. "It's gonna look real funny, you not bein' there with that big rodeo cowboy comin' all this way to see you."

Niki felt her spine stiffen. "Don't start on me, Cleavon," she begged. *"Please."*

He sighed. "I won't, but you showin' up would sure save Rosie's bacon. She's out there makin' a fool of herself and hopin' against hope you'll do this one little bitty thing for the town."

Niki rolled her eyes. "That's what you said when you talked me into taking that Cowboy Dream Girl title. Cleavon, I'm twenty-seven years old which is too old for all that beauty contest nonsense. I'm afraid I've done just about all the little bitty things I can for this town."

With a wave, she moved away to wash down tables that didn't need it. She'd taken only a couple of steps when the door opened and her sisters walked in. With a groan, she bowed to the inevitable and went to meet them.

"What'll it be?" she asked cheerfully, just as if they were regular customers. "Cleavon's got a special on the Sorry Burger, if you're hungry."

Dani and Toni exchanged exasperated glances and Dani said, "All we want is you, Nik—out there acting nice."

"This is as nice as I get these days." Niki spun away.

Toni jumped in front of her. "Rosie's dyin' out there, trying to act as if everything's all right. She was so sure you'd change your mind."

"Just because I always have before, after being brow-beaten and bullied for a couple of weeks? I'm sorry but I can't do that again."

"But this guy is *cute*." Dani joined the offense. "I mean, *really* cute. At least come out to meet him and let the photographers take a couple of pictures."

"What part of no way, never, forget it don't you people understand?" Niki wrung her hands together. "This is making me crazy! My own sisters..." She let her voice trail off mournfully.

Dani, seemingly undeterred, fixed Niki with a level gaze. "Okay, we tried. If you really don't want to do this, I don't suppose we should give you any more flack about it."

"But on the other hand..." Toni tried to turn the tide.

"No, really," Dani said sanctimoniously. "I guess Niki's happy in her own little rut. Far be it from us to try to shake her out of it."

Toni frowned. "I wouldn't say she's in a *rut*, exactly."

Dani's brows soared. "No? She works at the ranch and here and that's it. She doesn't date—"

"I certainly do," Niki said huffily.

"When's the last time you had a date?"

"I...I don't know. When's the last time you had sex? Oh—!" Niki clapped a hand over her mouth. "I'm sorry, that was way out of line."

"This morning about six." Dani's expression was challenging. "And I liked it!"

"I'm sorry," Niki said again, miserably. What had possessed her to say such a thing? Sex wasn't a topic often on her mind....

"I repeat, when's the last time you went out on a date?"

"Who was it with?" Toni chimed in, apparently catching on.

"I don't remember. There, are you satisfied?"

"Not hardly." Dani pursed her lips. "I just felt it necessary to support my contention that you're in a rut. You need something to shake you out of it—not for the good of the town but for your *own* good."

"I am not in a rut." Niki recognized the defensive edge in her tone and hoped her sisters didn't. "I'm *happy* with my life."

"Really? Hiding out here at the Sorry Bastard or back at the ranch, a big fish in a little pond? No husband, no kids—hell, Nik, you don't even have a dog of your own!"

"Dani!" Niki stopped short, surprised by the laughter bubbling in her throat. "Oh, all right," she grumbled. "You've made your point."

"Will you at least think about it?"

"Yes, I'll think about it. Now go away and let me do my job."

She watched them leave, feeling the weight of melancholy settle upon her shoulders. If her life was as dull as they made it sound, was she then equally dull? Maybe if she wasn't reasonably pretty, she wouldn't have any friends at all.

Talk about a depressing thought....

NIKI'S SISTERS eventually reappeared and were last in line to meet the guest of honor. Ignoring the crowd of men and boys still clustered around Clay in a loose but attentive semicircle, the dark-haired one stuck out her hand and said, "I'm Dani Keene Burke."

The one with lighter hair added, "Toni Barnett. We're Niki Keene's sisters and we thought we..." She looked uncomfortable. "...uh...we owed you an explanation."

Mayor Rosie heaved a gusty sigh of relief. "Thank heaven y'all showed up," she said. "I've been dreading havin' to do this alone."

Clay, who knew exactly what they were talking about, smiled warmly. "I'm pleased to meet you," he said. "Will your sister, Niki, be joining us soon? We've kept the photographers waiting as it is." He gestured toward the two men sitting on the back edge of the bandstand, talking quietly.

"That's just it." Dani looked pained. "I'm afraid...she won't be coming."

Clay raised his brows. "Because...?"

"Because..." Dani looked at Toni who looked at Rosie who looked distressed.

Finally the mayor did her reluctant duty. "Niki says she doesn't want to be in the contest," she admitted faintly.

"You're kidding."

"I wish. She didn't actually even enter—somebody else did it without checking with her first," Rosie explained uneasily. "She wasn't real happy when we surprised her with the news at our big Fourth of July bash but we were kinda hopin' she'd change her mind."

"Being a finalist in a big national contest isn't exactly an insult," he pointed out.

"We all told her that," Toni said. "We *want* her to do it—everybody in town wants her to do it." The other two nodded agreement. "It's just that she's stubborn. The more we push her, the harder she digs in her heels. Now we're at the point where I don't think anything could change her mind."

Clay smiled. "Well," he drawled, "maybe I can just come up with a way if I think on it real hard...."

THE FRONT DOOR to the Sorry Bastard flew open and in walked the sexiest man Niki Keene had ever seen in the flesh. He was followed by half—the younger half—of the males in this part of Texas. Two photographers trailed along behind.

Laughing, talking, the men pulled together several of the tables and hauled up chairs with much scraping of chair legs. Dylan Sawyer thumped a fist on the tabletop and shouted, "Beer all around, Niki! We got us a celebrity here we're tryin' to impress...my buddy Clay Russell."

"Coming right up, Dylan." Being careful to avoid looking at the "celebrity," she hurried to the bar where Cleavon was already drawing beer into frosty mugs.

This might be harder than she'd expected. She'd

been unable to stop thinking about Clay Russell after only one very low-key glimpse of him. Now he was back full force, confident and charismatic as if he'd just been fooling the last time.

He *had* been fooling, she realized, picking up the tray of beers. He'd been incognito, undercover—spying on her, in fact.

She distributed the beers, smiling and friendly while trying to keep her gaze averted from his. She didn't want anything to do with this man. He was a threat to her...boring existence, if her sisters were to be believed.

But when push came to shove, she just couldn't carry it off. Placing a cold mug of beer before him, she slowly raised her gaze until it met his amused one. "Goodness me," she said in her best Texas-belle accent, "I sure never expected to see *you* again, Mr. Russell. The last time you dropped in, you said there was nothing around here you really wanted."

His smile was dazzling. "I was wrong," he said softly. "I want *you*, Niki Keene..."

She caught her breath because one look and she knew that. He couldn't change anything by adding...

"...*you*, competing to be Mother Hubbard's Queen of the Cowgirls. You'd be perfect for the job."

"I already have a job." Hands trembling, she placed the last beer in front of Dylan.

"But this one is part-time and you've got a flexible

boss who'd be delighted to give you all the time off you want."

He sounded so reasonable that he made her feel *un*reasonable, although she knew she wasn't. "Mr. Russell, I don't think you quite understand—"

"Clay," he inserted with a smile. "Call me Clay."

"*Mr. Russell,*" she repeated firmly, "You don't know me well enough to offer career guidance."

"Maybe not, he countered, "but I know you well enough to be your benefactor whether you appreciate my help or not. This isn't an opportunity that comes along every day."

"Thank heaven." She gave him her sweetest smile. "If that's all, gentlemen..."

"Not nearly."

The air sizzled between them. Disconcerted, Niki took a hasty step back. This was not going her way. "Excuse me," she said breathlessly. "I've got to get to work."

"Not so fast. Kidding aside, there's something I really have to talk to you about." He rose.

She kept backing away. "I told you—"

"I know, but I've traveled a long way to talk to you and this won't wait. Is there someplace private we can go?"

"I don't want to go someplace private with you."

A suggestive smile curved his lips. "What are you afraid of, Niki?"

Dylan, who had been watching with overt curiosity, laughed. "Niki's not afraid of nothin' or nobody," he boasted. "Tell him, Niki!"

She *had* said that a time or two, most particularly when some customer was making a pest of himself. It was hardly applicable now since she was absolutely terrified of Clay Russell—or more precisely, terrified of the confusion she felt in his presence.

Even so, she lifted her chin. "You don't look all that dangerous to me," she said, looking straight at Clay. "Am I to assume that you won't leave me alone until I hear what you have to say?"

The smile broadened. "Yes, ma'am, that's about it."

"Then follow me, cowboy." Turning, she led the way toward Rosie's office at a fast clip. The sooner she got this over with, the sooner he could go away and quit messing up her mind.

CLAY FOLLOWED HER through the maze of tables and out into the hall, admiring the swing of her hips beneath a long denim skirt. Her shoulders in chambray looked stiff and filled with tension. This he could understand because he felt a little tense himself.

He wasn't sure why, because he liked women, all women. He liked 'em tall and short, beautiful and otherwise. But this woman was different—not because she was gorgeous enough to stop traffic but because of some invisible signal she seemed to send out to every man in the vicinity. He didn't for a moment think he was the only man aware of this but apparently not many of them had been able to get close enough to her to explore the possibilities, thus her touch-me-not-I'm-a-goddess aura.

The more she resisted, the more he wanted her...to stay in the contest. For her own good, he told himself righteously, and he pretty much believed it was true.

Pretty much.

She opened a door marked Private at the end of the hall and stepped aside to let him enter first. "Rosie won't mind," she said, "if we don't take too long, that is."

A dire warning that she didn't intend to let this drag out. He almost laughed.

Twin desks, one neat and one messy, dominated the room. Clay sat down in a wooden straight-backed chair and crossed one ankle over the opposite knee, regarding her whimsically.

She closed the door and leaned against it as if it provided some degree of safety in a hostile situation. She took a deep breath and her breasts rose beneath the soft blue fabric, kicking off all sorts of erotic images in his mind.

"Please," she said, "say what you have to say. I'm listening."

"All right." Suddenly sober, he nodded. "First tell me why you want to drop out of the contest."

"I don't *want* to drop out, I *am* out," she said firmly. "I was never in. I didn't enter this or any other contest and I never would. People are always doing this to me and it's got to stop somewhere. Here, for example."

"Your other titles were just a warm-up for this one," he said, all seriousness now. "This one can do you and your town and your ranch a whole lot of good. It's a win-win situation."

She said nothing, just looked at him impassively with those beautiful long-lashed blue eyes.

"No come back?" he inquired.

"What's the point? I'm waiting for you to say something I haven't already heard."

He had to laugh at that. "I did say I had some points to make," he admitted without shame. "Niki, you're standing against the tide but if that's what you want to do, I don't suppose there's anything anyone can do about it. I do wonder, though...if you could make one tiny little concession, or maybe two."

She stared at him, a beautiful mass of suspicion. "Like what?"

"Like...could you wait a while to formally withdraw? I'll pass on your decision to Mother Hubbard but I'd appreciate it if you'd hold off on officially dropping out. How about this—let it stand and if you don't change your mind, just don't show up for the finals next month."

She puzzled that one over. "What good would that do anybody?" she asked finally.

"It'd give Hard Knox time to revel in your re-flected glory," he said. "That would please people around here, don't you think?"

She hesitated. "I know it would." With a sigh, she finally gave up whatever sanctuary the door had provided. Stopping in front of his chair, she frowned down at him. "What's the point—really?"

"Mother Hubbard—that's Eve Hubbard—is...let's call her eccentric. This contest was her idea and she doesn't want anything to go wrong.

If you withdraw, she'll have to bring in the first runner-up to get twelve contestants and she doesn't think that will look good. On top of that, she thinks you've got a good shot at the title and—"

Mistake. Her expressive face closed down.

"Lighten up," he said quickly. "If you're not there on D day you won't have to worry about who wins. Eve will get all caught up in the contest and forget all about you."

She seemed to be thinking this over and she wasn't smiling. "What's the second small little concession?" she asked after a moment.

"We've got a couple of photographers out there who have been waiting all afternoon to take a few pictures."

"I don't like having my picture taken."

"Who does?"

Her blue eyes widened. "I thought you would, as

often as I see your picture in magazines and news-papers."

So she'd noticed. He didn't dare smile but that's what he felt like doing. "Nah," he demurred, "I don't like it, either. Makes me feel like a sissy but that's part of my job."

"It's not part of mine."

He raised his brows at that. "Really? Then why is one whole wall of this place devoted to pictures of you?"

She blushed, really blushed...a rosy glow suffusing those high cheekbones with wonderful color. "That wasn't my idea," she said stiffly.

"But you went along with it. Why not go along with this? Those photographers out there have a job to do so how about letting them do it? Just a couple of shots— It'll only take a few minutes. As for dropping out of the contest...just don't put anything in writing quite yet. Okay?"

"Clay..." Anxiety creased her smooth forehead. "This doesn't feel right to me."

"It feels *way* right to me." He wouldn't let her avoid his steady look.

After a moment, she sighed. "Okay, a few pictures. That's all. But you have to realize that really is all. No contest, no Queen of the Cowgirls—which would be an oxymoron anyway because I'm not a cowgirl. Will you accept that?"

"If that's your final word, I'll have to."

"You won't harass me about it?"

"I never said that." Laughing, he stood and took her arm before she could avoid it. Her flesh felt warm and firm beneath his hand. "Shall we face the music together?"

She didn't look as if she liked the sound of that but she nodded.

So he'd won the first round. Somehow he thought there'd be plenty more rounds to come before he won the war.

SHE'D BEEN on the verge of agreeing to anything to get away from him. Within the confines of the office, she'd felt smothered, overwhelmed by his charisma.

She really didn't know why, unless it was a simple case of sexual attraction. Simple! Bite your tongue, she scolded herself.

So here they were, approaching the two photographers sitting at a table in the back of the room engrossed in conversation. They looked up with identical questions on their faces.

Clay nodded. "The lady's ready to have her picture taken," he said as cheerfully as if the delay had been mere minutes instead of hours.

Tom Martinez, the *Hard Times'* veteran photographer, grinned. "No sweat. Niki's worth waiting for." He gave her a friendly wink. "She's one of my favorite subjects."

"I can see why." The other photographer looked

her over appreciatively. "Ed Davis," he introduced himself. "Shall we get to it?"

So they got to it, as did everyone else in the Sorry Bastard. Niki posed against her "tribute wall," she posed at the front door, she smiled for close-ups and generally accommodated their requests however trivial. They ended up in front of the bar, behind which beamed her employers, Rosie and Cleavon Mitchell.

"Hoist her up on the bar there," Ed directed Clay. "Let's try a little cheesecake."

Niki took a step back. This was getting real old real fast. "I don't think that's such a good idea," she objected.

"It's a great idea," Rosie interjected. "Sit right here, beneath the neon sign with our name on it."

"Rosie, your name is not Guilty—"

Clay moved so swiftly that he took her breath away. His hands felt strong and sure on her waist and he lifted her as if she weighed nothing at all. Her hands covered his for support and she gasped, finding herself held high in the air and staring down into his dark, dark eyes.

He wasn't laughing. The connection between them was so strong that it felt like some magnetic force drawing them together. Instead, with a reluctance she could feel, he sat her on the bar and dropped his hands as if touching her had burned his fingers.

As it had burned her.

She swallowed hard and moistened her lips for another stagey smile. The two photographers were climbing around over tables and chairs, trying to get the angle they wanted. Both frowned as if dissatisfied with what they saw.

Tom gestured with his camera. "Get in the picture, Clay," he instructed. "Right up close...that's good, but closer. Put your arm over her knees...."

Clay gave Niki an apologetic look, then did as instructed. She sat with her feet on a barstool while he faced forward, away from her. Slowly he lifted his left arm and slid it over her thighs, letting his hand hang down on the other side.

Niki felt as if she were burning up. His body heat seemed to enter straight into her veins and spread like lava. Without thinking, she slid her hand over his shoulder and leaned forward.

She must have startled him for he looked back sharply, his eyes questioning. She gave a helpless little shrug and appealed to the photographers.

"Will you just take the picture and be done?"

"We are done," Ed said. "Thanks. Uh...Clay, do you plan to be around for a while or are you heading out now? I'd like to shoot a few more rolls if you're gonna be here."

Everybody looked at Clay.

Whose grin became suddenly teasing. "I'm gettin' kinda fond of the Keenes," he said. "I'd like to hang out at the Bar-K for a while, if they have room for me."

And his arm tightened over Niki's knees to keep her from jumping off the bar in her astonishment and probably breaking her neck.

4

INTO THE STUNNED SILENCE, Dylan let out a wild *ya-hoo!*

"Room for *you?*" the young cowboy said rhetorically. "Do we ever!"

Niki jumped down off the bar. This situation was getting out of hand fast. "No, we don't," she exclaimed. "Every cabin's taken for the rest of the season but if you want to stay over at the XOX, I'm sure they could find room for you without too much trouble."

"Thanks, but I'd prefer to stay at the Bar-K," he dismissed her compromise. "Actually, it's just what I've been looking for."

That statement suggested multiple possibilities and she risked a glance at him. "Meaning...?" Suspicious, so suspicious.

"Meaning someplace to hole up for a while and heal."

That's right, he'd been hurt; she remembered reading an item about his injury in the newspapers. That's why he had the time to wander all over the countryside driving women crazy.

"You don't look hurt to me," she said, giving in to her natural suspicion. In fact, he looked fine—*very* fine.

"I'll take that as a compliment." He glanced around at the small crowd of onlookers still remaining. "Why don't we sit down and I'll explain everything."

"I'm sorry." Reaching behind her waist, she untied the bow of her apron. "It's time for me to go now but Lisa will be glad to take your order."

"Are you going to the ranch?"

"That's where I live."

"Then I'll just follow you there and we can talk about it a little more. Maybe your grandmother will be more sympathetic to my plight than you are."

Was he laughing at her? She couldn't be sure. "You'll be wasting a trip," she said stiffly.

"Nah, you won't," Dylan put in eagerly. "There's always room in the bunkhouse, Clay."

Clay laughed, his dark eyes mischievous. "Thanks for the offer but I had something a little...cozier in mind. I'll give a holler, though, if all else fails."

"It will," Niki said defensively. She turned to her two wide-eyed bosses behind the bar. "I'll see you two days after tomorrow." With a slight wave, she turned toward the doorway leading to the employees' lockers where she'd stowed her purse.

Clay followed directly behind her so she stopped. "No, seriously, don't waste your time."

"Somehow I don't think I will be." He cupped her elbow with his hand. "But if I am, I won't blame you, Niki."

"Promise?" She shivered. Just his slightest touch made her feel intensely alive. Thank heaven there truly were no vacancies at the Bar-K. "It's a free country, so I don't guess I can stop you."

She didn't think she could stop him even if it *wasn't* a free country.

AS LUCK—all of it bad—would have it, everybody was up at the Bar-K ranch house when they pulled into the yard. Family members mingled with guests on the big front porch and all the rocking chairs were in motion. A big pitcher of lemonade, glasses, and a tray of cookies were arranged on Granny's portable serving cart. The older children chased each other around the ranch yard while toddlers tried to con cookies from the unwary.

Niki felt the weight of attention on her as she walked up to the porch with Clay at her side. At least he wasn't touching her, which made her situation a little easier to bear. Granny came down the steps to meet them.

"Niki, honey, I'll just bet this is Mr. Clay Russell." She stuck out her hand. "I'm the grandma around here, Tilly Collins by name."

"Glad to meet you, Mrs. Collins." His approving gaze lifted and he looked around appreciatively.

"Nice place you've got here. I was hoping you could find enough room for me to hang around for a few days. This is the last of twelve stops and I'm kinda worn out."

Just like that, no lead-in, no set up, just a blunt statement. Niki gave him an annoyed glance. "I *told* him we're booked solid."

"But under the circumstances," Dani cut in, "I'm sure we could find *some* place to put him."

"Dylan Sawyer suggested the bunkhouse," Clay offered, his wide mouth quirking up at the corner.

Dani grinned. "I think we can do better than that." She turned to her grandmother. "Now that Toni and I have both moved out, there are two empty bedrooms in the house. Why couldn't Clay stay here?"

Niki nearly choked on her indignation. "That's impossible!"

"Why?"

Everyone looked at her with varying degrees of surprise, with the exception of Clay who looked as if he knew exactly what had occasioned her outburst.

"B-because—the house is a private residence, at least the upstairs is. We can't let just anybody move in with us."

Granny patted Niki's shoulder. "This fine young man isn't just anybody," she said. "We've got lots of room with both your sisters married and gone, plus, it isn't every day we have a visit from a celebrity. I know how you avoid the limelight, honey, but this will be real good for the business."

His celebrity had nothing to do with the apprehension she felt but she was almost tongue-tied in her attempts to explain.

Granny went on. "Look around at our guests and you'll see what I mean."

Reluctantly, Niki did. Men, women and children of all ages stared down avidly at the little gathering at the bottom of the porch steps. She was sure that no more than half of them even knew who Clay was but he had the kind of personal magnetism that drew attention. If he was around long enough to turn on all that charm, they'd probably end up asking for lifetime leases on Bar-K cabins.

She gave them the ironic smile tugging at her lips. "I don't think he wants to stay here to publicize the ranch," she suggested.

He raised his brows. "You scratch my back, I'll scratch yours. I'll also be glad to help out in any way I can."

"In that case," Granny announced, "consider yourself one of the family." Grasping his arm, she drew him up the steps. "Folks, I'd like you to meet a very special guest who'll be staying here at the Bar-K. Mr. Clay Russell is a rodeo champion and he's going to be spending a few days with us. Clay, this is—"

While Granny introduced him to all the eager

guests, Niki poured herself a glass of lemonade and lingered in the background. After a while, Dani joined her.

"So what's the status of the contest?" she asked.

Niki shrugged. "No change. He's suggested that I not do anything official, just not show up."

"Why?"

"I don't really know. Something about replacing me—it didn't make too much sense but I don't suppose it would hurt me any to accommodate him."

Dani glanced at her sister sharply. "He's a guy who makes you want to accommodate him."

"Which means what?" Niki shot back. She didn't like to think she was that transparent in her reactions to him.

Dani looked surprised. "Just that he's a charmer—don't bite my head off." She frowned. "Nik, what are you so uptight about? I've watched you getting more and more tense—ever since the Fourth of July, now that I think about it. Are you okay?"

"As okay as I can be, considering that my very own sisters think I'm as boring as my life."

"We never said that. We just said you needed..." Dani sighed. "I don't know, some kind of adventure, I guess. Some excitement! But how can you have any excitement when you spend all your time working and protecting yourself from admirers?"

"It's hardly that bad," Niki said.

"Then prove it. Kick over the traces, do something unexpected, have some fun."

"Is this your subtle way of saying without saying it that I should stay in the Queen of the Cowgirls contest?"

Dani laughed. "No, silly, that's my way of saying Clay's here right under your nose. Go after him, because he's a one-man adventure if I ever saw one." With a suggestive wink, she walked away.

Niki frowned after her sister for a moment, then turned away and entered the house. Go after Clay? She'd have to be crazy to even think about it. She'd be no match for him.

Accustomed to frequently tongue-tied admiration, Niki was used to being in charge where men were concerned. In her secret heart, she'd longed to be approached by a man who'd treat her like an equal and not a goddess, who'd look beyond the surface to find the woman.

Now one had done just that and it threw her for a loop. Clay wanted her to compete in what was in essence just another beauty contest, but at the same time, he wasn't in awe of her. If anything, she got the feeling he wouldn't be surprised if *she* were in awe of *him*.

He was a big rodeo champ, as good-looking as a movie star and national spokesman for a famous clothing company. He was photographed and fêted all the time so he certainly wasn't going to be over-whelmed by a local femme fatale.

So why wasn't she plotting and scheming this very moment to work her wiles on him, instead of picking up a paring knife and reaching for potatoes that needed peeling for dinner? The answer to that was very simple.

She was afraid that...no, she was *sure* that she wouldn't have a prayer of getting the best of him. If the price of adventure was a broken heart, she wasn't interested.

DINNER THAT NIGHT was a riot. The more dudes that hung on his every gesture and laughed at every word he said, the more expansive Clay became.

He should have been ashamed of himself...but he wasn't. Generally speaking, he enjoyed his celebrity. Hell, he'd worked hard enough for it so he should. But he never enjoyed it more than when he could relax and be himself, the way he was doing now. The dudes were great, the Keenes were great, and he had a feeling this was going to be one of his better moves...assuming Niki eventually came around.

Waiting out the laughter, he glanced at her. She didn't seem to be listening, just playing with the food on her plate and looking serious. God, she was gorgeous, but so cautious. What had happened to make her that way?

She reminded him of a princess in a tower, waiting

for the prince to ride up on a white horse and awaken her....

Awaken her. A shiver of anticipation shot down his spine. He would be that prince, he thought with utter certainty. He would make her loosen up enough to laugh and...and love....

"Then what happened?" the teenage kid at the next table inquired. "Did you figure out what you were doing wrong or—?"

Clay pulled his thoughts away from Niki and went on with his tale of rodeo life. But when she rose quietly and carried her dishes through the swinging door into the kitchen, he was aware of it. And when she came back in toting a huge white coconut cake he was aware of that, too.

In fact, he seemed to sense every move before she made it. Which boded well for a more...intimate relationship.

"JUST TREAT ME like any other ranch hand," Clay said again, nodding for emphasis. "I'll be glad to pay the going rate for dudes, but I'll pay extra if you'll let me get out there and *work*."

Niki couldn't believe her ears. "Are you kidding?" she demanded. "I thought you were injured."

"I was, but I'm coming back. Working will be one way to gauge when I'm all the way back and ready to get into the arena."

"Makes sense to me," Granny said. "Shoot, there

are some dude ranches where the guests do all the work. We're not ready to go that far here, but there's no reason you shouldn't do whatever makes you happy."

Niki's heart jumped into her throat. She didn't even want to *think* about what would make him happy.

Solemnly he said, "Thank you, ma'am."

Granny yawned. They were seated alone in the Great Room; all the guests had wandered off to bed and it was after eleven o'clock. "It's been a long day," she said. "Niki, hon, could you show Clay his room and tell him where everything is? I'd better get along to bed or I'll never hear that alarm clock tomorrow."

Niki had to bite her lip to keep from protesting. The last thing she wanted to do was show Clay *anything*. But she nodded and murmured, "Of course. Clay, if you'd like to get your things..."

"Come with me." Rising, he held out his hand.

"I'll wait here," she said, pulling back.

"Chicken." He looked after Granny, rising out of sight on the staircase. "I don't bite."

"I do." Standing without touching his outstretched hand, she marched past him to the screen door and out onto the porch. The night air enveloped her, soft and tender. A full moon shone down, turning night to day.

"Nice night."

His voice, right in her ear, made her start and jump away. "Y-yes," she agreed, hurrying down the steps to the paved walkway. Pace accelerating with every step, she was nearly running by the time she reached his pickup truck.

He hauled a duffel bag out of the truck bed and swung it onto his shoulder. "Shall we run back to the house now?" he asked, a note of humor underlying his steady voice.

She couldn't help a rueful chuckle. "I suppose we could do that." She leaned against the truck door.

He stepped in front of her. "Maybe we better. Because you look just about good enough to make me forget myself, standing there in the moonlight like that."

She straightened in alarm. "Really, Clay—"

"It's true." He gave the bag a shove back off his shoulder and it hit the ground with a dull *whump!* "Why are you so uncomfortable with your good looks, Niki?"

"Who said I am?" She was grateful for the silvery shadows which must have hidden the heat rising into her cheeks.

"It's obvious."

He touched her cheek with his fingertips. Pressed back against his truck, she had no recourse but to stand fast and hope he couldn't feel or sense her embarrassment.

"You're gorgeous, but you don't enjoy it."

"P-pretty is as pretty does," she murmured, giddy from being so close to him and from his touch, however light. "They say I look exactly like my mother, and that didn't do much to help her have a happy life."

"Tell me about your mother." He trailed his fingers down her cheek, to her shoulder. Then his hand curved warmly around her neck, sliding beneath the heavy hair.

She felt completely within his power, somehow forced to answer although she didn't want to. Licking dry lips, she spoke hesitantly. "Everybody said she was the prettiest girl in Elk Tooth, Montana. S-she was flighty and impetuous and still very young when she met my father."

"I sense a sad story coming up here." He caressed her nape, then threaded his fingers into the mass of hair.

She nodded, intensely aware of his massaging touch. "She was seventeen and he was forty-something. He married her, got her pregnant and took off before my sisters and I were born."

His brows arched. "All of you?"

"We're triplets."

"Wow."

"Wow. Anyway, she died when we were still little and Grandma took us in. We never knew our father or anything much about him until he died a few years ago and he left us the Bar-K." She made an unhappy little grimace. "That was the only decent thing he ever did for us—maybe the only decent thing he ever did in his life."

He slid his hand from behind her neck and lifted her chin. "But you're only...what? Twenty-two or twenty-three? I don't see much of a resemblance between your life and your mother's."

"I'm twenty-*seven*, much too old for this beauty contest silliness."

"You're *kidding!*"

"I see you're not interested in older women. A break for me," she added dryly. "Why don't we go back inside now and I'll show you—"

"No, Niki, let me show *you*."

Holding her chin steady, he lowered his mouth to hers. His lips felt cool and soft. She knew she should break away, shake off the lethargy spreading through her limbs, but somehow she found herself incapable of motion.

She'd known she'd feel exactly this way when he kissed her, and had never for an instant doubted that he would, eventually. She had felt such a connection to him, so drawn to him.

But not so soon! Pressing her hands lightly against his shoulders, she tried to find the strength to push away...and failed. Even with her eyes closed, she felt overwhelmed and consumed by his physical presence. If he wanted to deepen the gentle brush of his mouth into something more, she knew she wouldn't be able to—

"That you over there in the shadows, Niki?"

At Dylan's question, she thrust Clay away from her and stepped quickly to the front of the pickup.

"Yes, it's me." She had never heard her own voice sound like that, all husky and throbbing.

"Just wanted to be sure everything is—oh, there's Clay with you. Sorry I bothered you folks."

She never saw him during the entire exchange, just heard his voice and then his footsteps receding into deeper shadow. Whirling to confront Clay, she snapped, "Why did you have to do that?"

"Kiss you?"

"No, *that* I understood. Why did you have to make sure Dylan saw you?"

"What's the matter, afraid you'll lose your virgin-goddess reputation if you're seen kissing a man?"

"That wasn't a kiss and we both know it. That was an invitation to dance and I think I'll pass."

He leaned down to hoist his duffel bag back onto his shoulder. "Dance, huh? I guess you could call it that."

She walked back to the house, intensely aware of his footfalls behind her. Once inside, she closed and locked the door before leading him up the stairs.

"You can have Dani's old room," she said, point-ing to a door opening off the hall. "The bathroom's there—" She pointed to another door. "—but I'm afraid you'll have to share it."

"With you?"

"That's right. Granny's in the master suite and she has her own bath, but everyone else has to share."

"There is no 'everyone else,' only us."

That sounded much too intimate for comfort. "Yes, well..." She half-turned. "There are fresh towels behind the door and anything else you need, just open drawers until you find it. I'll see you tomorrow, I guess."

"Don't sound so happy about it." *He* certainly sounded happy enough. "Uh...Niki, one more thing."

She hesitated, the hair at her nape prickling. "Yes?"

"You never did tell me what you have in common with your mother, except that you look like her."

She turned slowly back to face him. "I don't know you well enough to talk about my mother. Some things...my sisters don't even know. I'd appreciate it if you don't mention this again."

"I'll bet you would." He swung his duffel bag to the floor. "Good night, Niki. Just in case you wonder...you look just as good in the moonlight as you do the rest of the time. Don't forget, tomorrow I'm just another ranch hand." Touching fingers to his forehead in a little salute, he turned away.

She watched him go, thinking, Yeah, sure—the all-around champion rodeo cowboy of the world is going to be a dude wrangler? What he was going to be, she was sure, was a headache.

She was only half right. Clay was not only an immediate and enormous hit with everyone he met, he was a hard worker to boot. He could do it all, handling stock as well as he handled people...as well as he'd handled Niki.

Gritting her teeth, she turned away from the sight of him giving a roping lesson to a twelve year old from New Jersey. What a tale the boy would have to tell his friends about the rodeo champion!

"Wanna go for a ride?"

His whispered invitation caught her completely by surprise and she started violently. She hated the quiet way he moved around, often catching her off guard.

"No," she said, "I don't want to go for a ride." She added hastily, "Thanks anyway."

He frowned. He had on a buttoned bib-front blue shirt, and his Wranglers and boots were old and well-worn. With his white hat shoved to the back of his head, the dark hair spilled out over his forehead rakishly.

"Ah, c'mon," he wheedled. "Everybody's going, so you won't have to worry about—" He winked. "—you know."

She did, darn it, and her cheeks warmed. "There

will be no more 'you know' between us," she said firmly. "That's not what I'm talking about."

"Then...?"

"I don't ride."

"You don't ride...what?"

"Horses."

He stared at her, no longer kidding around. "Why not?"

"I don't like horses."

"Get outta here!" His eyes widened. "Everybody likes horses."

"That's your opinion. *I* don't like them and I don't ride. Ever. At all."

"But..."

She could hear the wheels turning in his head and she said, "So how can I aspire to something so lofty as Queen of the Cowgirls? The answer is—I can't!"

She left him standing there staring after her. For the first time, she felt as if she'd won a round.

CLAY FILLED a glass with water from the kitchen sink and drank deeply. Across the counter, Grandma grinned at him.

"Have a good ride?"

"Yep." Pretty good, anyway. "Uh...Mrs. Collins, why doesn't Niki like horses?"

Grandma's smile fell away. "Oh, that."

She pursed her lips, examining him closely. He felt

as if she saw right through him somehow, but he held his ground.

She seemed to make up her mind then. "When she was just a little tyke, say four or five years old, she got stomped real bad by a loco stallion that jumped a fence to get at her. The poor little thing nearly died. Then several years later, her sisters decided to get her over her fear of horses by putting her up on an old plow horse. I'll be darned if that animal didn't fall into a ditch and nearly kill her all over again."

"Poor little Niki." He sucked in a slow breath and changed the subject. "She said she's like her mother."

Grandma's glance sharpened. "They sure favored each other, if that's what you mean."

"There's more to it than that."

"That's not for me to say." Grandma reached into a cabinet and withdrew a large stainless steel bowl. "I'm not quite sure what all these questions are for, Clay."

He shrugged, pretending to be casual when he didn't really feel that way at all. He was still caught up in a tiny girl running afoul of great big horses at every turn. "I'm still hoping she'll compete for Queen of the Cowgirls," he said finally.

"Well, she won't." Grandma pulled out a canister of flour.

"You sound mighty sure about that."

She shrugged. "I've known her her entire life," she

said reasonably. "She doesn't like people staring at her and she sure doesn't like horses, so we got a little problem goin' in."

"Yeah, but—"

"Clay, I agree with you," Grandma cut him off with a smile. "She's just about the prettiest little thing I've ever seen and she'd be a great Queen of the Cowgirls—in name only. But she's not gonna do it, so if that's why you're here, you're paddlin' the wrong canoe."

He finished the water and placed the glass in the sink. "You may be right, but I'm not ready to give up quite yet."

"Suit yourself. Just don't blame anybody when you come up empty."

"I won't," he promised.

He wouldn't have to. Eve Hubbard would do it for him.

5

NOTHING WAS TOO MENIAL for Clay to tackle cheerfully. He whistled while cleaning horse stalls, sang while washing dishes outdoors at the steak fry, did a little impromptu tap dance while lugging dirty sheets to the laundry truck. He'd been at the Bar-K less than a week and already seemed as comfortable as if he owned the place.

Watching through the kitchen window, Niki smothered a wistful smile. What a shame they hadn't met under other circumstances, but she could never look at him without remembering he was here for reasons other than the usual.

The truth of the matter was, he wanted something from her—maybe more than one something. She knew instinctively that he still hadn't given up on her participation in that blasted contest, and perhaps not on a more personal relationship.

Neither of which was going to pan out for him, but it didn't do any good trying to tell him that. Apparently he was one of those men who just set his sights on his target and bulldozed ahead.

She turned from the window. "I've got to go to

work now, Granny," she sang out, drying her hands before hanging her apron on a hook. "Don't wait up for me."

From somewhere deep in the house came her grandmother's muffled acquiescence.

In the parking lot out front, she climbed into her battered old car. Thrusting the key into the lock, she twisted.

Nothing happened.

She tried again with the same result.

"It could be the battery."

He'd done it again; crept up on her to speak practically in her ear. "Can't be," she said, her heart banging against her ribs. "I got a new one less than a month ago."

"Whatever you say, ma'am." He flashed that crooked grin. "I can give you a ride into town, if that's your pleasure. Then I'll come back and see if I can figure out your problem—your car's problem, I mean."

She hesitated, chewing her lip, then sighed. "Thanks, I guess I'll have to take you up on that." She opened her car door and climbed out. "But do you know anything about cars? Usually I have Jack come take a look but he's awfully busy these days."

"Your brother-in-law," he translated. "Let me take a shot at it before you bother him. I grew up on a ranch and something always needed fixing so I might be able to handle it."

"Okay, and thanks again."

People, animals and now vehicles—was there nothing this man couldn't handle? A little voice told her that if she wasn't careful, she just might find out how truly versatile he was.

"I KNOW I'VE BEEN here for a week, Eve." Clay shifted the telephone handset to the other ear. The woman not only wanted the impossible, she wanted it *right now*. "Yes, I'm making progress—slowly. She hasn't officially withdrawn, has she? Then I'm doin' my job."

Through the window he could see the bonfire in the ring of rocks near the pool. Unerringly he picked out Niki's silhouette as she moved around the perimeter of the leaping flames, assisting dudes.

She'd been surprised when he'd fixed her car—and it really *was* the battery. Actually, he'd liked her being without a vehicle because it gave him an excuse to drive her to and from work. That way he knew—

"Clay Russell, are you listening to me?"

He yanked the telephone earpiece away, then gingerly replaced it. "You don't have to bust my eardrums," he said. "Yes, I'm listening. Uhh...what were you saying?" The plaintive strains of a harmonica reached his ears, shortly followed by the unsteady strumming of a guitar.

"That if you don't get it together I may have to

come way down there and see what's going on for myself," Eve snapped.

Damn, he didn't want her doing that. It would seriously get in his way with the elusive Ms. Keene. "No point," he said quickly. "I'll keep you informed but you gotta remember, there's a lot going on around here."

"There's a lot going on around here, too, and you don't hear *me* whining."

She hung up on him. He shrugged and replaced the handset. Eve Hubbard was not the dude-ranch type. He'd be very surprised if she made good on her threat.

His mind wasn't on his eccentric boss, however, but upon the festivities going on outside. Quickly he left the house and crossed the yard to the strains of "Home on the Range." Joining the revelers, he sidled up to Niki. She gave him a guarded glance and kept on singing.

The matronly lady from Tulsa slid over with a smile to give him a seat next to her on a fallen tree trunk worn smooth by many bottoms. He sat down just as the song ended.

Niki led the applause. "That's wonderful, Mr. Hammer. Do we have anyone else who can play a musical instrument or lead us in song?"

They all looked around, but no hands rose until Clay cautiously inched his own just about ear-high.

The lady from Tulsa laughed and pointed at him.

"Clay's got some hidden talent," she announced. "C'mon, Clay, tell us, what do you do?"

He rose with feigned reluctance. "I play a little guitar," he said modestly, "even sing a little now and then."

Applause led him forward, but it wasn't coming from Niki, who looked at him with a frown on her lovely face. Clay accepted the guitar thrust at him and strummed the strings lightly.

He'd learned to play guitar from one of the hands on his uncle's Oklahoma ranch and he knew he wasn't half bad. His singing was a notch below that, but what he lacked in ability he made up for with enthusiasm.

Without further ado, he launched into a spirited version of "I Ride An Old Paint," a popular cattle-driving song from the previous century. To his surprise, most everyone joined in the chorus: "Ride around, little dogies, ride around them slow..."

Finishing the song, he spoke above soft strumming. "Next time you go out to punch cows, that's the song you sing, folks." He spared a quick glance at Niki and suddenly all the glib words flew right out of his head. She was looking at him with an expression he'd never seen before, part astonishment and part approval.

He liked it. Not wanting to risk the moment, he launched quickly into "Git Along Little Dogies," which nearly everyone knew. He followed that with

"Goodbye Old Paint" which pretty much turned into a solo. When he hit the last chord with a flourish, everyone applauded.

"More! More!" shouted the little lady from Tulsa.

"Just one, then." Clay drew a deep breath and sang the opening words to "My Dearest Annie May," a love song by anybody's standards. He sang it straight to Niki, a cowboy's lament that although he wasn't good enough for his pure and noble lady-love, he would nevertheless "swim the deepest ocean or ride the rankest hoss" to win so much as one tender glance.

The final mournful notes drifted away and the Tulsa lady sighed audibly. "My goodness," she said, fanning herself with one hand, "if any cowboy ever sang to me that way I'd—I'd give him more than a tender glance, I swear I would."

Everyone laughed except Niki. She still had that strange expression on her face and Clay figured he'd just have to find out what it meant.

NIKI GLANCED at the man walking beside her to the kitchen, his hands as full of dishes as her own. Still off-stride as a result of his unexpected performance, she said politely, "You play the guitar very well."

He gave her a slanted glance. "How'd you like my singing?"

"You play guitar very well."

They laughed together. Then she said, "You surprised me."

"How's that?" Awkwardly he held open the kitchen door for her to enter first.

"I never dreamed you'd be musical. You're a man of many talents."

"And you ain't seen the half of 'em." Placing his armload of pans and bowls on the counter, he took the tray from her hands and put it beside the other things. "Niki, I want to ask you something."

Her nerve endings tingled with alarm and she backed away. "What?"

"To go riding with me."

He looked serious in the bright fluorescent lighting. So engrossed was she in staring at him that it took a moment for his words to register. When they did, she said incredulously, "On a *horse?*"

"That's the usual way of it on a ranch."

"No." She said it flatly and turned away.

"But—"

"Clay, drop it." She whirled around to face him again. "I'm deathly afraid of horses and that's the end of this discussion."

"One or two bad experiences shouldn't—"

"You don't know anything about it, so please don't push me. If you want to get along with me..."

"I want more than that, my dearest Annie May." He stepped up close to her, just short of touching. "I want a tender glance." His gaze caught and held hers. "For starters."

"No you don't. You want me to change my mind about that contest. But I'm not going to, Clay. You're wasting your time."

He swayed an inch or two closer. "I don't think so."

She shrugged as if it didn't matter. "It's your time. If you want to waste it…"

"I don't. I want every minute of my life to count, and yours, too. Niki—"

"Niki, are you still in there? I'm about to turn off the lights—"

She skittered away from him and spoke toward the closed door leading into the Great Room. "I'll do it, Granny. You go on to bed."

"All right. Good night, then." And after a slight pause, "Good night to you, too, Clay."

His low chuckle sent chills down Niki's spine.

"Good night, Mrs. Collins. Sleep tight."

They stood in silence for a few moments, the earlier intimacy shattered. Then he said, "If you change your mind about riding with me, I can guarantee that nothing will go wrong. I mean, with proper caution—"

"Guarantee? You can't guarantee any such thing. Horses are big, stupid animals. They can hurt you without even trying."

"But—"

"No, Clay." She shook her head with finality. "There's nothing you can say or do that will change my mind about that."

But as it turned out, there was plenty he could do to reinforce her preconceived notions on the subject.

IF THERE WAS A HORSE on the Bar-K Ranch that looked reliable, it was the old gray mare named Bessie. That's why Clay was caught flat-footed when she shied, reared, and tumbled over backwards. He almost managed to roll clear, but not quite. The horse landed partially on top of him, rolled over and staggered up again.

Fortunately, this happened in the corral where the dirt was soft from the pounding of many hooves.

Unfortunately, it happened just as Niki climbed up the pole corral to say something to him.

The mare stood there trembling and Clay just lay there gasping. The saddle horn had hit him in the side and he had a sinking feeling that something was either broken or seriously bent.

Before he could get himself together enough to rise, Niki hopped over the top rail and dropped onto the soft dirt of the corral. Running to him, she knelt at his side. She bent over him, her pale face framed by satin ribbons of black hair that teased his cheeks.

"Clay! Oh, my God! Are you all right?"

His head cleared a little, although he still heard a

ringing in his ears. "I'm fine. Just give me a minute to...catch my breath."

Gently she lifted his head and cradled it on her lap. With tender hands, she swept his tousled hair away from his face. "You could have been killed," she said in a trembling voice. "After all you said last night about horses...."

"There's nary a horse that can't be rode and nary a rider that can't be throwed," he proclaimed, interrupting her tirade with one of his uncle's favorite homilies. "It was an accident, Niki. Old Bessie didn't mean anything by it. She was scared, that's all." He turned his head enough to see the mare, trembling in the corner with her head drooping. "I think she feels as bad as I do."

"Is that supposed to make *me* feel better?" She glanced around frantically. "Do you want me to call the doctor? Maybe you need an ambulance."

"Nah, I'll be all right." He struggled up to a sitting position—and it *was* a struggle. Stabbing pains made it difficult for him to catch his breath. "But on the other hand...it probably wouldn't hurt to have a doctor check me out."

She still knelt next to him, her expression disapproving. "I'll drive you into town."

"I can drive myself." Then he realized that maybe he couldn't, and even if he could, why deprive himself of the pleasure of her company? She wouldn't be going into the examining room with him, after all. "All right," he said, giving in, "I'd appreciate it."

"That's more like it." Standing, she offered a hand to help him rise.

He accepted her help, using the other hand to brace his ribs as he struggled to his feet. "This isn't the first time I've been thrown," he said, striving for lightness. "It happens to everyone from time to time, but getting piled is no reason to give up horses."

"It's also no reason to start with horses, either." She wedged her shoulder under his arm and wrapped her own arm carefully around his waist, glancing up with quick concern. "Am I hurting you?"

She could have been killing him, but he probably wouldn't have said so and risk having her move away. Draping his arm over her shoulder, he managed a shaky smile. "You, hurt me?" he teased. "Not hardly!"

She rolled those beautiful blue eyes and led him haltingly toward the cars out front. By the time they got there, he'd recovered sufficiently to make it on his own, but no way was he going to tell *her* that.

"OKAY, DOC, give it to me straight. I can take it."

Seated on a plastic-covered examining table and bare to the waist, Clay faced Doctor Wilson, who'd just finished his examination. The doctor did not respond in the same kidding manner.

Instead he frowned. "If you don't quit all this non-sense," he said bluntly, "You're gonna end up dead or crippled. Is that what you want?"

His brusque speech went through Clay like nails on a blackboard. "Doc, it was an accident."

"I can believe that. Nobody sets out to get the stuffing knocked out of him."

"But..." Clay touched his ribs gingerly. "I'm feeling a whole lot better. I don't see how it can be as bad as you say."

Doc turned on the water in the stainless steel sink. "You're right, nothing's broken," he said, washing his hands. "But it's not so much what you did today as it is what you've been doing for years. You got off lucky this time, but there's so much residual damage that any injury is serious."

The doctor's words made Clay distinctly uncomfortable, especially considering the fact he'd heard variations of the same tune before. "C'mon, it's no big deal," he said in cajoling tones. "Just tape me up and send me on my way."

"I can do that," the doctor agreed, "but a warning goes with the tape job." He rummaged through the contents of a glass cabinet. "I can see how this was just an accident. I'm no cowboy but I've ridden enough to know that even a good horse can be spooked by a shadow or confused by a gnat. A bad horse, on the other hand...or a bad bull... Well, my advice to you, mister champion cowboy, is to give 'em *all* a wide berth if you want to live a long and productive life."

And that was all he said on the subject.

It was enough.

"So what did the doctor say?" Niki asked, rising anxiously from her chair in the waiting room. She tossed aside the magazine she'd been holding as opposed to reading.

Clay grinned. He was moving much more easily than when they'd arrived. "He said I'm a damn fool and he should be examining my head instead of my ribs."

"Sounds to me like he has a point." She felt the tight knot of worry in the pit of her stomach begin to loosen.

"Yeah, that's how it sounded to me, too." He cocked his head. "Aren't you going to come over here and put your arms around me and lead me to the car?"

She raised her brows, amused in spite of herself. "I hadn't intended to."

"You did when we came."

"But then I thought you were *really* hurt."

He sighed. "Are you one of those women who only like wounded men?"

"Nope. I'm one of those women who only like smart men. Smart men don't mess with big mean animals."

He laughed. "Niki Keene, you sound like a broken record. Come on over here and give me a hand which I may or may not need but will enjoy regardless."

And she, entranced by his cheeky smile, meekly did his bidding. Because like he said, she'd enjoy it regardless.

THE DOCTOR'S OFFICE shared parking with the drug store next door. On the verge of climbing into the car, they spotted Dani's husband Jack heading for the Hard Knox Pharmacy.

"I wonder who's sick?" Niki said. "Jack! Yoo-hoo!" She waved. "Over here!"

Jack changed his path and trotted over to them. "What's up?" he asked, removing his hat to wipe perspiration from his forehead.

"Not much," Niki said vaguely, for which Clay was grateful. "You?"

Jack's jaw tightened. "Dani sent me in to pick up some stuff for Elsie's gums. Kid's teething and I don't know who's suffering most, her or us."

"Poor baby." Her expression turned to one of concern. "Is there anything I can do?"

He shook his head. "Can't think of a thing. Maybe pray that tooth will break through is all." His gaze rose to meet Clay's and he grinned suddenly. "So how's life at a dude ranch?"

"Not too bad. They're feedin' me good." Clay rubbed his belly, careful not to jar his strained ribs.

"Yeah, they do that all right." Jack turned away, then wheeled back. "I guess you two saw that picture in the paper."

"What picture?" Niki asked.

Jack's grin nearly split his face. "The one that says something to the effect that you'll make a great Queen of the Cowgirls and the king obviously agrees."

"The king? Sorry, I don't get it."

And then she did; Clay saw it in the sudden widening of those blue eyes, in the way they darkened almost to purple.

"Oh, no," she breathed.

"Oh, yes. You can check it out at the *Hard Times* office." He tapped his hat brim. "I gotta get a move on or Dani will skin me alive. I left her home alone with a screaming kid and that doesn't usually bring out the best in her."

Clay waited patiently until Niki finally turned to him, her expression grim. "Do you now anything about this?" she demanded.

"About teething kids?" He shook his head. "No way."

"I'm not talking about Elsie, I'm talking about a picture in the newspaper."

He shrugged. "That's what the pictures they took

of us were for," he pointed out reasonably. "I can't say I'm surprised."

"What about that great Queen of the Cowgirls stuff? Did you have anything to do with that?"

"Niki, that's the point, remember? Only you, me and Eve know you're not going to go through with it."

She gritted her teeth. "I suppose you're right, but I still want to see what kind of hogwash is being put out about me. Do you mind if we drop by the newspaper office on the way back to the ranch? I'd like to see that picture."

"Not at all. You're drivin'. I'm just along for the ride."

The look she gave him plainly said she didn't believe that for a minute.

"OH, NO!"

Niki stared at the photograph on page one of the *Hard Knox Hard Times* with dismay. She'd never imagined anything so bad.

Or so good, from the photographer's point of view, for there was an intimacy between the two attractive people that fairly leaped off the page. And the explanation below the photo practically said she had the title in the bag.

Clay, peering over her shoulder, gave an approving grunt. "Nice," he said.

"*Not* nice." She folded the paper and stuck it under her arm. "I feel like a fraud, Clay. I'm not going to be the Queen of the Cowgirls and we both know it."

"Yeah, I guess so. It's really a shame, though."

"It's *not* a shame. It's reality."

"Nobody wants reality in these situations," he corrected her gently. "People want the fantasy—the beautiful girl who has it all including the handsome hero, or me, if that's all that's available."

She gave him a wry smile. "Mother Hubbard didn't hire you because you frighten babies," she said in tart tones. "You'd qualify as a handsome hero in anybody's book."

He looked startled by her comment. "Hey, thanks." He gave her a slight bow. "You gotta admit we look good together. Real good."

"That's your opinion," she sniffed. "All I see when I look at that picture is fraud, fraud, fraud."

"You mean because you don't like horses?"

"I mean because I hate, loathe and despise horses."

"Hon, that's just a simple little...a simple little hang-up. If you'd just give me a chance, I can help you get over it."

"Did it ever occur to you that I don't want to get over it? That I'm happy as I am?"

"No, seriously, listen. You need at least a passing familiarity with horses if you're going to—"

"Don't say it!" She faced him with clenched fists. "You're totally wrong."

"You don't even know what I was about to say."

"I sure do. You were going to say *a passing familiarity with horses if I'm going to be Queen of the Cowgirls.* Which I'm not. I don't know why you can't leave it alone."

He looked offended. "You've got me all wrong. I was going to say *if you're going to live on a ranch.*" And he gave a self-satisfied nod for emphasis.

That took the wind out of her sails, but only momentarily. "I don't believe you, but that doesn't matter," she said. "I will never, ever, as long as I live get near another horse." She turned toward the car parked at the curb, tossing back a final challenge over her shoulder. "And you can take that to the bank!"

Maybe, he thought on the way back to the Bar-K, but he wasn't making any bank deposits on it just yet. She was protesting too much. If he could just get her over her phobia about horses—

Granny opened the front door and stuck her head out. "Telephone, Clay!"

Had to be Eve; just what he needed to cap a bummer of a day.

His guess was right. His boss's voice grated on his nerves.

"So, report already! Has she agreed to do this?"

"No." He spoke softly because the phone was in

the Great Room and lots of people, including Niki, were milling about. "Why this sudden urgency?"

"Have you seen the pictures?" she countered.

"You mean in the local paper? Sure."

"Then you should know why—you two are dynamite together. I can sell more denim with those two faces than my suppliers can crank out. You two are a magic couple, big guy. Pure magic."

Her ravings made him distinctly uncomfortable. "Yeah, the pictures were all right, I guess."

"So don't keep me in suspense. Are you making progress?"

"What kind of progress?" *Mistake!*

"Ha-ha-ha," she said, her tone dry and cynical. "Does that mean you have a personal as well as professional interest in our future queen? Watch your step, Clay. I don't want your personal life getting in the way of my professional life. Got that?"

"Yeah, I got it, but I'm gonna ignore it." He had to unclench his tight jaw in order to speak. "You're paying me to push Mother Hubbard duds. What I do with my free time is my own business."

"Unless it slops over into *my* business," she corrected him. "Now tell me you haven't given up."

"I haven't given up. Hell, I don't know *how* to give up, even when it would be the smart thing to do."

"That's my boy," she said with pride that crackled over the line. "Make Mother happy and Mother will make you happy...very, very happy."

He hung up the phone and stood there for a moment, thinking that although money was nice and absolutely essential in many cases, it still wasn't the most important thing on earth.

Which was an entirely new concept for Clay Russell.

6

CLAY DIDN'T SLEEP worth a damn that night.

His ribs ached, sure, but that wasn't the real reason. Eve's call had him all riled up. He didn't like having someone looking over his shoulder all the time. Never had.

Especially when the subject was Niki, he wanted a free rein. He didn't want her slipping away any more than Eve did, but not because her image would sell a ton of denim.

The truth was, he wanted Niki to win the title so she'd have to spend the next year making personal appearances with him—and personal *non*-appearances, too. He figured that would give him plenty of time to discover her flaws. He needed to do that because as things stood now, he knew nothing about her that was off-putting in the slightest. Check that: her unfriendly attitude toward horses was a definite downer. He was going to have to do something about that, but *what* would take some thought.

Staring past frilly curtains out the window of his second floor bedroom, he looked into the yard illuminated by moonlight. This was a great spread, he thought. Niki seemed so much a part of it, so very much at home, but it was all illusion.

Anyone who feared horses as she did couldn't possibly belong on a ranch. If he wanted any future with her—

The hair on his nape stood straight up in alarm. What was this about a future? He wasn't ready to settle down with one woman and wouldn't be for years and years—maybe never. But that didn't mean he wasn't interested in feminine companionship.

Yeah, that's what he wanted, what he needed; a little of Niki's feminine companionship.

Preferably in a horizontal position.

To hell with that. If he kept thinking in this vein he'd never get to sleep. Climbing back into the bed, he told himself that all he wanted from Niki was...Niki.

BY THE TIME dawn broke—and he was awake to see it when it did—Clay had decided what to do first. He'd enlist everyone he knew in his campaign to convince Niki she should go for the title. The first person he saw upon whom he could try his new strategy was Jack, who'd come over to talk to Grandma about Elsie's teething problems.

"We saw the picture on the front page," Clay remarked as he walked beside Jack to his pickup truck.

Jack gave him an impish grin. "Good one, I thought."

Clay nodded. "Niki takes a great photograph."

"Yeah, and she's not exactly a dog in person."

That drew a laugh. "You sure as hell got that right. It's a shame she's still determined to sit this one out."

Jack frowned. "When I saw the picture, I assumed she'd changed her mind."

Clay shook his head. "It's a real shame, too, since there's some great prizes, not to mention a contract with Mother Hubbard. Travel, money, lots of new clothes, adventure...."

"I dunno. Niki likes to stick kinda close to home." Jack reached the pickup and draped an arm over the open window. "It'd do her good to get out in the world for a change instead of hiding her light under a bushel in little ol' Hard Knox, Texas."

"You'd think so." *Take it slow and careful, Russell. Don't rush him.* "Why does she do that, do you suppose?" he asked aloud.

Jack shrugged. "Hell, I don't have a clue. You know how women are. They get the damndest ideas in their head and we're just supposed to pretend they make sense."

Clay laughed. "Is that how it is with you and Dani?"

"Hell, yes—and Simon and Toni are the same way. It's like lovin' a whirlwind, gettin' tangled up with a Keene woman. But you know what?" Jack jabbed an elbow into Clay's already sore ribs. "They're so danged cute you can overlook a lot."

He climbed into the truck and hung his arm and head out the window. "I'll talk to Dani about this," he promised. "I think it'd do Niki a lot of good to kick over the traces and get out in the world where everyone can see what a special lady she is." He touched his hat brim and drove away.

Clay just stood there frowning. He hadn't exactly been talking about Niki "kicking over the traces." As far as he was concerned, the fewer men who knew what a "special lady" she was, the better.

He was going to have to rethink his strategy here.

SUDDENLY it seemed to Niki that everyone was on her case all over again. It had to be that picture in the newspaper. She fumed as she hacked at the pile of potatoes that would magically turn into potato salad for the trail ride and cookout tonight. She'd drive the supply truck to the site where the chuckwagon was permanently installed, then help with the cooking and serving.

Dobe Whittaker wandered through the back door into the kitchen. The old cowboy looked agitated and his first words confirmed that state of mind. "Where the hey is that grandma of yours, girl?"

Accustomed to his blunt way of speaking, she shrugged. "She said something about checking on that leak in the Jesse James cabin, but that was hours ago."

"Guess I'll just have to go door to door 'til I find

her, then." You'd have thought he meant state to state, judging by his level of annoyance. He started to turn, then hesitated to squint at her. "What's all this cowgirl stuff you're mixed up in, Niki? Everybody's talkin' about it."

"They are?" Dismayed, she frowned. "What is everyone saying?"

"That you'd be a danged fool to pass this up. You done more for less—like that cowboy sweetheart thang. They had you runnin' all over the State of Texas, as I recall, and all you got out of it was sore feet."

"Since when are you so interested in what I do and don't do?" She regarded him with suspicion.

"Since it's turned that grandma of yours into a regular tyrant," he said readily. "She was hard enough to get along with before this come up and now she's worse."

Niki disregarded that last comment. Dobe and Granny had never gotten along, not since the day they met. Of an age and a perfect match for Mr. and Mrs. Santa Claus, they mixed like water and oil. Everybody else just ignored the friction and went on about their business.

As Niki did now. "Granny's about the only person who hasn't tried to twist my arm about this," she said.

"It ain't 'cause she don't want to. Guess she just figures you're dead set on cuttin' off your nose to spite your face and there's nothin' she can do about it."

"Well, for goodness' sake!" Flushed with annoyance, Niki threw her paring knife into the bowl of potatoes. She was *not* doing this to spite her face. Then she remembered what the point really was. "It's Clay," she said flatly. "He's got everyone all worked up about this."

"Not me, he don't. As I recollect, Dylan was the first one talked to me about this."

"It's none of Dylan's business."

"Shoot, Niki." The old man gave her a pitying look. "What's wrong with him wantin' to know somebody famous? It'd make him and everybody else happy and not hurt you a lick." He straightened, his hand going to the doorknob. "And speakin' of Clay Russell..."

Her antenna tingled. "Yes?"

"He is one helluva man, if you want to know the truth. He's as hard a worker as I ever seen and he can do *everything*—I mean, every gosh darned thing that comes up. Considering how he grew up, that's no big surprise, but—"

"How did he grow up?" Niki asked quickly. He'd certainly never spoken about personal things to *her*.

"On a ranch in—wait a minute, if you wanna know, ask 'im. Now I gotta go find me a grumpy old woman who's gonna chew my head off for lettin' them cows get loose in her posy patch." Shaking his head in anticipation of the coming battle, he let himself out and closed the door behind him, in deference to the air-conditioning.

Niki sat there for several minutes, thinking about all Dobe had said. Was she really cutting off her nose to spite her face? She didn't think so, but she'd been under so much pressure lately....

Clay was making her crazy, yet the thought of him giving up and going back to wherever he'd come from made her less than happy. She wanted to be around him and she *didn't* want to be around him. She wanted to be in his arms and she *didn't* want to be in his arms.

He had her tied up in knots and as far as she knew, it didn't matter to him one way or the other. This had never happened to her before...well, only once...and she didn't like it one little bit.

Rising, she crossed to the enormous refrigerator and pulled out mayonnaise and relish. She was going to have to do something about this—about Clay, not about the gossip going on behind her back. Because Dylan was simply a mouthpiece for his idol.

All her troubles led back to one very sexy cowboy with an irresistibly cheeky grin.

ONCE EVERY WEEK during dude season, the Bar-K featured a big trail ride, ending at a permanently installed chuck wagon on Lookout Point, the highest spot on the ranch. All the hands went, everyone but

Niki, that is, who wasn't climbing on a horse for anyone or anything.

So when she wasn't scheduled to work at the Sorry Bastard, she took over Sheila Owens' duties as chief cook and bottle washer: helping Grandma prepare the food, loading it into the back of the pickup, driving it to the site, unloading and completing preparations on the spot.

Hard work, but well worth it because this was probably the most beautiful spot on the ranch, she thought as she took boxes and baskets of supplies off the truck and stowed them in the rear of the chuck wagon mounted on a concrete base. By the time the riders appeared, she'd have a fire leaping in the fire ring and another in the cooking pit below the grates where the steaks would soon be sizzling.

Content, she looked out over the small valley. This ranch would be heaven on earth if she just didn't have to confront the "horse question" nearly every day. The move here from Montana had proven to be a good one. Two of the three Keene triplets had found love and romance. The third...hadn't.

Tight-jawed again, she turned back to her duties. Soon the jingle of spurs and the creaking of saddle leather heralded the approach of the trail riders and she pasted a bright smile on her face. Clay would be among them and she had a few things to get straight with Mr. Russell, once and for all.

"COULD YOU USE a little help?"

Clay spoke softly in Niki's ear, but she still jumped as if he'd grabbed her. She gave him an annoyed glance over one shoulder, her hands still deep in the tin tub of soap and water.

"I wish you'd quit doing that," she said.

"Doing what? Trying to help?"

"Sneaking up on me that way. It always scares me to death."

"I'm not sneaking. I guess I'm just naturally quiet." That thought made him laugh.

She smiled in response, however reluctantly. She looked beautiful standing over that pan of dirty dishes, framed by the setting rays of the sun. A long wisp of hair blew across her mouth and she tried to push it aside using the back of her wrist the way women do.

"Let me do that." Intending to brush the strand of black hair away, he touched her cheek...his fingers skimmed the corner of her mouth, setting off a shower of sparks in his bloodstream. His body leaped to throbbing readiness in an instant. Slowly he scooped up that silky lock of hair and smoothed it back behind her ear.

It was one of the most suggestive moments he'd ever experienced and he felt it in exquisite detail: the softness of her skin, the vitality of her hair, the look of vulnerability in eyes widening to reveal dark purple depths. He wanted to take her into his arms right then and there, bury his head in the fragrant curve of her neck and hold her—

"Oh, my." She said it softly, breathlessly, turning back to the pan of soapy water.

He let his hand fall aside; difficult to do, requiring all his considerable willpower. "You haven't answered my question," he said.

"You asked a question?"

He laughed. "I asked if you needed any help."

"You don't want to do dishes." Her voice had recovered a bit of its usual spice.

"Says who?" He unbuttoned the cuffs of his turquoise shirt and shoved the sleeves up. "You'd be astounded at what I want to do."

"You know," she said, "I probably would."

"Then step aside and let me do my stuff." He put his hands on her hips and exerted the very slightest pressure.

She didn't step aside, but she didn't tell him to keep his hands to himself, either. "D-don't you think you should be over around the campfire for the s-singalong?" she stammered.

"They don't need me. You do."

She caught her breath. "I'm used to handling cleanup alone. Besides, you're a guest and—"

"That's debatable. But just for argument's sake, let's say I *am* a guest. I should get to do what makes me happy." A great grin escaped. "At least, within reason."

This time he simply lifted her bodily off the ground and set her back down to one side. Taking her place before the wash pan on the back of the chuck wagon, he plunged his hands into the water and felt around for dishes.

Glancing at her over one shoulder, he added, "Besides, you told me when we arrived earlier that there was something you wanted to talk to me about."

She bit her luscious lower lip, absently drying her hands on the towel tied around her waist for an apron. Finally she said, "This probably isn't a good time. We can talk about it later."

"Whatever you want," he agreed. "Did I tell you what a good meal that was?"

"Yes." She smiled. "But I don't mind hearing it again."

He took a calculated risk. "Who'd ever think a woman so good-looking could cook, too."

Her smile faded. "Don't you expect a good-looking woman to be *smart* enough to cook?"

"I expect her to be smart enough to figure out how to *keep* from cooking."

"I happen to enjoy it, when I have time." She lifted her perfectly rounded chin to a challenging angle.

"An old-fashioned girl, huh?"

"I don't know that I'd...." She looked suddenly disconcerted. "Maybe." She took a couple of steps away, twisting the towel between her hands. "Thank you for doing the dishes, Clay."

"My pleasure."

"You constantly surprise me." The words burst out as if she could no longer hold them back.

"Meaning you had a lot of preconceived ideas about what a pro rodeo rider would be like?"

"I suppose so." She looked distinctly uncomfortable admitting it.

"As I had a couple of preconceived ideas about what the holder of a dozen or more beauty titles would be like," he said gently. "Niki, we could put all the preconceived ideas aside and start over."

"Could we?"

Their glances met and held, his probing and hers somehow defenseless. The intimacy of the moment thickened, gelling into an unexpected significance.

"Niki—"

She caught her breath and whirled away. "I need to refill a few coffee cups, if you'll excuse me." She raised her voice. "More coffee, Dobe?"

"Not me, but that grandma of yours'll take some. And bring lots of sugar. Might sweeten up her disposition!"

The hooting and hollering covered any confusion Niki might have felt as she passed around the campfire circle refilling tin cups with the stout brew. Clay watched with a kind of resignation.

She was as skittish as a filly unaccustomed to the saddle, but every time he approached he got a little closer before she scampered away. Soon there'd come a moment when no ready excuse would come to her rescue and when that happened...

Whistling, he turned his attention back to the stack of dirty dishes. When that happened, he'd be ready.

Hell, he was ready now.

IT WAS AFTER ten o'clock by the time they all got back to the ranch, dispersed the dudes, and put everything away. The cowboys straggled into the bunkhouse and the dudes to their cabins. Only Grandma, Clay and Niki remained in the ranch house.

Niki held out the remains of the campfire coffee, still in the huge enamel pot. "Anyone like a last cup before I clean the pot? I could heat it up—"

The telephone rang.

Grandma frowned. "My stars," she said, crossing to the wall phone. "Who can that be at this hour? I sure hope one of our guests doesn't have an emergency." She picked up the handset and said, "Hello?"

Niki glanced at Clay. "How about you?"

"No, thanks. I've had about enough coffee for one day." He draped his long frame over the counter and stifled a yawn. "I think I'll go out and check that swimming pool pump in a minute. It's been soundin' kinda funny for the last couple of days. If it's going out, I'd like to catch it before we end up with a swamp out there in the front yard."

We. He'd said *we* just as if he had a stake in what happened at the Bar-K. She shivered.

"All right. Thanks."

His gaze narrowed. "I thought maybe you'd like to go with me."

The tension always there between them went up another notch, until the air fairly hummed with it. She swallowed hard. "Not a good idea."

Granny hung up the phone with a clatter that interrupted what was happening. "My word, that was Dani and she's just frazzled."

"What's wrong?" Niki was instantly alert.

"It's Elsie. She's still trying to cut that tooth and she's fussed and cried until her mama is about ready to pull her hair out."

"And such nice hair, too," Clay offered with a smile.

Niki's heart sank and something much more dangerous rose in its place: anticipation. "You're going over there," she said, a statement and not a guess.

Granny nodded. "I have to give that girl some relief. Jack's in San Antonio on business—Dani thinks he just had to get out of the house before that child drove him crazy. At the very least, I can stay up with Elsie and send Dani off to bed."

"You mean, all night?" Niki nearly gasped the words, her alarmed gaze flying automatically to Clay.

He'd turned away; was that to hide his expression?

"Yes," Granny said. "It'll take a while to get Miss Elsie calmed down, assuming I do. There's no point in me driving all the way back here in the dead of night. You two don't mind."

"Well...well, no, but—I—" Niki was sputtering and stammering again so she just shut up.

Clay turned back around, all business. "Don't worry," he said cheerfully. "I'll take care of everything."

That's what Niki was afraid of, but she saw no way to voice her concerns under the circumstances.

Still Granny hesitated. "I hate to ask this, but Clay...I wonder if you could..."

"Anything." He spoke expansively, spreading his arms wide as if things really were going his way. "Name it."

"Could you drive me over to Dani's house? I don't trust these old eyes to drive at night. She can bring me home tomorrow."

The way the air whipped out of Clay's sails was almost funny. Niki would have laughed had she not been so overwhelmed with relief...mixed with a certain amount of disappointment.

She could almost read his thoughts: *But she'll be asleep by the time I get back. I won't have a chance to—*

"Sure, Mrs. Collins." He'd pulled himself together. "Glad to."

"Thank you, dear. Now I'll just go grab a couple of

things and be right back. I'll meet you at the front door."

She hurried out of the room. For an electric moment, Niki and Clay stood there looking at each other.

He smiled slowly. "You look like you just dodged a bullet," he said.

"I don't know what you're talking about." Head high, she turned toward the sink and poured out the dregs of the coffee. Maneuvering the pot beneath the faucet, she turned on the water hoping he'd take the hint and leave.

He spoke directly in her ear in that way he had that simultaneously scared and excited her.

"Liar."

"I do not lie," she said stiffly. Occasionally she might stretch the truth or omit pertinent information, but that was all.

"I can prove it."

She felt his hands settle over her shoulders and then the warmth of his lips pressing against the curve of her shoulder between her neck and the collar of her shirt. Her heart stopped beating in that instant and she stood there, stunned, her breathing labored and her nipples tightening.

The flick of his tongue against her skin made her gasp and lean back against his chest. Somehow she thought she felt his heart banging in a frenzied rhythm, but she might only have heard her own. He slid one arm around her and his hand closed over her breast. She groaned and let her head fall back while delicious sensations flooded through her. This was going much too fast; her head was spinning.

It was time for good sense to reassert itself. Why get all worked up and excited—make that *more* worked up and excited—when he would be leaving in a matter of minutes?

She straightened with an enormous effort, her hand closing over his where it rested on her breast. "No," she murmured raggedly, "Stop! You've got to go."

"But I'll be back." He squeezed gently at the rounded flesh.

"I won't be waiting."

"Niki, you know you want—"

"I won't be waiting. This is ridiculous. I don't want this." At last she found the strength to push his hand aside and step away. "You'd better go. Granny will be waiting."

For a moment she thought he'd refuse and then he said, "I *will* be back."

"I know, and I'll be asleep when you get here so please try not to make a lot of noise."

He gave a bark of laughter that seemed to settle him down. "Asleep. Yeah, sure you will." He turned to the door. "Sweet dreams, Niki. I'll see you tomorrow, then."

And he was gone.

7

THE INSTANT Clay and Grandma closed the front door behind them, Niki made a dash for the stairs and the safety of her own bedroom. Even if she wasn't asleep when he returned—to be honest, there wasn't a chance in *hell* that she'd be asleep when he returned—he wouldn't know that.

At least she hoped with every fiber of her being he wouldn't.

With trembling hands she threw off her clothes, twisted her long straight hair up into a loose knot and stepped beneath the stinging spray of the shower. This should help—a rush of chilly water designed to snap her back to reality.

But then she looked down and saw the pebbled tips of her breasts and nearly collapsed against the shower stall, remembering the fleeting pressure of his palm—

Stop it, she raged at herself. She didn't want a sleazy affair, even with a man as desirable as this one. A relationship with him could never go anywhere. It would break her heart, and in the end she'd be worse off than she was now.

If that was possible. Her entire body thrummed with unfulfilled desire. She'd never wanted to make love to any man the way she longed to make love to this one—to let this one make love to her. Not even Steve Miles, her first love, had filled her with this kind of overpowering passion.

She turned off the shower and stepped out onto the bath mat. She shared this bathroom with him and his razor rested next to the sink, his soap-on-a-rope hung from the showerhead, his toothbrush next to hers on the rack. His presence overwhelmed her, even when he wasn't here.

She'd never been overwhelmed by a man before and it scared her. Wrapping the big bath towel around her body, she scurried across the hall and into her own room. Slamming the door behind her, she leaned against it as if fearing pursuit.

IT TOOK slightly less than an hour to deliver Grandma to Dani's door and drive back to the Bar-K. Fifty-five minutes of torment for Clay Russell, he thought as he pulled to a stop in the ranch house parking lot.

The brief scene in the kitchen had left him plenty worked up. The memory of how her breast had fit the curve of his hand was imprinted on his memory, making him groan and twist uneasily on the pickup seat. He'd been so close to his goal....

Jeez, his goal wasn't simply to get her into bed—at

least, it wasn't supposed to be. He was here to convince her to compete for the Queen of the Cowgirls title. The other was just a...diversion.

Of course, if they were intimate she might realize more quickly the benefits of spending the next year in his company. He could modestly hope so, at any rate. But he wouldn't use sex to get her to change her mind, he vowed. The passion with which he desired her didn't have a damn thing to do with Mother Hubbard or her Duds. It had to do with the electricity he'd felt the first time he touched her, with the mind-bending excitement of kissing her, with the tightening in his gut just thinking about her naked and wanting.

Taking a deep breath, he crawled out of the truck and looked up at her window. The entire house was dark, he realized with a shock, except for the porch light which was always left on. He couldn't believe it.

Had she *really* gone to bed? If she had, so help him, he'd—

A flash of white behind sheer curtains caught his attention and he stiffened. In an instant, he realized she was up there watching him, knew she'd seen him arrive and now was dashing back to bed to pretend she'd been asleep the entire time.

Two could play that game...at least for a little while. *Let's see who breaks first,* he thought with rising spirits. Walking up the steps to the front door, he stood for a moment to compose himself before entering.

It was a battle of nerves now and she was dealing with a professional.

Let the games begin.

NIKI LAY in her bed stiff as a proverbial board. If he walked in now and saw her like this, he'd know damn well she was faking.

And he *could* walk in, if he took a notion. There was no lock on her bedroom door and even if there were, she wouldn't have used it. That would be nothing short of an admission of helplessness. No, she'd tough it out.

She heard his footsteps in the hall and waited for the sound to stop at her door. It didn't. Instead, he moved on down the hall and into his own room.

That was it? After all her worry and dread, he was just going on to bed?

No, he was just going to take a shower. The bathroom door opened and closed. Seconds later she heard the familiar rumble of water rushing through pipes.

Okay, then, when he got out of the shower he would cross the hall, open the door and slip into her room. She was sure of it. But forewarned was forearmed and she'd give him a piece of her mind if he pulled anything like that. Her blood pressure rose. Just let him try it!

He turned off the shower and she twisted her hands into the sheet. He'd be toweling off now...would he put anything on for the short trip across the hall? They were the only people in the house. Why bother with details at such a time?

Door hinges creaked open and she held her breath. The floorboards complained beneath his tread and she trembled.

The next sound she heard was the opening of a door—his door, not hers. She sat bolt upright in bed.

He wasn't even going to give her an opportunity to turn him down.

He can't do this to me! she thought wildly, casting about for some method of revenge. *He's got me all worked up and now he's going to ignore me?*

She was halfway to her door before she got hold of herself. Her first instinct was the wrong one: to blast through his door and *yell* at him. Oh, sure—*yell.* They'd end up doing something more than yelling, sure as shooting.

This was for the best, she tried to reason with her pounding pulse and outraged mind. Instead she'd go down to the kitchen, get a glass of cold water and... Throwing it in her face would probably do the most good, she thought willfully.

STANDING just inside his bedroom, Clay heard her quietly enter the hall and turn left.

His room lay to her right. She was *not* planning to pay him a visit.

He stood there for a moment in the darkness, gritting his teeth.

Then he opened his door quietly and padded down the hall after her.

NIKI DIDN'T NEED or want a light to navigate the kitchen. With unerring steps, she crossed to the big stainless steel refrigerator and paused with her hand on the door pull.

Then with a sigh, she leaned forward and pressed her burning forehead to the smooth cool surface. He had her in such a state that under other circumstances, it might have been funny.

Niki Keene, cool, calm and collected Niki Keene, the woman who never lost her head over any man, the woman always in control...

Yes, *that* Niki Keene, stood there wracked by a sexual hunger that had come at her out of left field. Fortunately, she'd found the strength to resist—or more like it, lacked the guts to follow her instincts.

By tomorrow, she'd be herself again. All she had to do was get through the night.

Opening the refrigerator door with a lurch, she peered inside. There in the back on the second shelf, she spotted a pitcher of lemonade left over from lunch. Leaning down, she reached inside.

"Need some help?"

His voice in her ear brought her bolt upright; if she'd had a weak heart, she was sure it would have failed. Whirling, she gasped a single outraged word: "You!"

"Who were you expecting?"

He stood there with a white towel wrapped around his middle. In the faint glow of the refrigerator light, he stared at her as if her long T-shirt was actually see-through chiffon.

"I was thirsty," she said inanely.

His dark brows quirked. "Sure you're not really hungry?"

"Clay..." She felt completely exposed, standing there in the dark room before an open refrigerator. Looking for a last ditch defense, she grasped at straws. "I know you're only here—at the ranch, I mean, not in the kitchen—to try to get me to change my mind about that contest. Don't you think making love to me just to get your way would be going a tad too far?"

"That's not why I intend to make love to you."

Intend, not *want*. She shivered. "In th-that case, I've got a question. Which do you want most, a celebrity cowgirl or a quick roll in the hay?"

"Can't I have both?" he asked plaintively.

"You can't have either." Straightening, she clutched the refrigerator door. "I have no intention of...getting involved with you."

"You're already involved with me." He reached

out, deliberately laying a possessive hand on her breast and looking straight into her eyes while he did it. "You want this as much as I do. Quit stalling, Niki. The time is now, right this minute, and you know it."

"Clay, no." It was a groan. Leaning slightly forward, she pressed against his hand. "You don't understand...."

"But I want to." He pulled her into his arms and kissed her.

She opened her mouth beneath his without urging, as eager to taste and savor as he was. He consumed her, controlled her. Somehow she found herself backed up against the small utility table next to the refrigerator. His mouth never left hers, even when he lifted her onto the edge of the wooden table. Spreading her thighs, he stepped close.

It took her a moment to realize that he intended to take her right here in the kitchen. She put her hands on his shoulders and tried to push herself away. "Clay, what—?"

"Easy. I won't hurt you. It'll be good."

Quickly and efficiently, he hauled her T-shirt over her head and tossed it aside. Stunned, she looked down at the pale gleam of her naked body barely illuminated by the light from the refrigerator. She'd never imagined anyone so adept at disposing of clothing.

Including his own, if the towel laying on the floor at his feet could be considered a garment.

He bent to her breast, drawing the pebbled nipple deep into his mouth. The manipulations of his tongue made her gasp, made her lean toward him and cradle his head in her arms. With each strong sucking movement, rich sensations radiated through her body, making her slick and ready for him.

He slid his hand between them, trailing his fingers up her inner thigh to touch her intimately. Exposed, vulnerable, she could only tremble beneath the sensual assaults of mouth and hand...and fingers, sinking deep into the moist recesses, withdrawing a little, plunging in again. Hot and throbbing before, now she felt the final shred of control slip away.

"Just a second," he panted, stepping back. "I've got to—"

"A condom?" She couldn't believe her eyes. "You came downstairs dressed in a towel and carrying a condom?"

He rolled the latex tube into place and reached for her again. "I had a feeling—" He dragged her hips to the very edge of the table. "—that I might get—" He stepped into her again, thrusting, his hands squeezing her buttocks and lifting her onto his erection. "—*lucky!*"

He sank into her to the hilt, and she felt against her cheek a gentle puff of air which accompanied his sigh of possession. Crushing her against him, he whispered in her ear. "I knew it would be this way."

"So...did I," she whispered back, curling her legs

around him and hanging on for what was already the wildest ride of her life. Her mind whirled and she felt a kind of breathless anticipation for what was yet to come. Carried away, she let herself soar.

He plunged and withdrew, again and again. She clung to him with arms and legs, letting him lift her higher and higher until she didn't think she could bear the rising hunger of her body another second. Her fingers convulsed, her nails scraping lightly over his shoulders and her head fell back. Gasping, she clung to him, afraid she'd fall, but at the same time supremely confident he'd catch her if she did.

The orgasm hit her like a tidal wave, bringing with it a kind of melting release that stole away what little breath she had left. Almost immediately he stiffened, groaned, slipped into the same hot languor that had already claimed her.

After a moment, he lowered her until her weight was once again supported by the table instead of by him. Still intimately joined, they clung to each other, the only sound in the quiet dimness the gradual lessening of heavy breathing. By the light of the open refrigerator door, she watched the slow relaxation of his features.

He lifted his head at last and looked at her with a faint smile that conveyed satisfaction. "Think we ought to close that fridge door? We can't refrigerate the entire Hill Country no matter how long we try."

She stifled a slightly hysterical laugh by pressing

her mouth against his shoulder. It was almost a kiss. When she could speak, she murmured, "Of all the things you might have said, that was the least expected."

A wary alertness touched his expression. "What were you expecting?"

"Something brilliant like...*gosh, I don't know what came over me.*"

"But I *do* know what came over me." He lifted her hand to his mouth and kissed her palm. "I've been wanting this for a long, long time—wanting you."

His words filled her with an unexpected warmth. "In the dark of night in the kitchen?" she teased.

He chuckled and began moving against her again. "What's the matter, too exotic for you?"

The feel of him inside her was electrifying. She couldn't believe she wanted him again so soon. "I...guess not," she choked out.

"I'm willing to give it a try in another venue, as the sports announcers say it." He spread her legs wider so that he could stroke the insides of her upper thighs with his palms. "How about we go upstairs...in just another minute or two?"

"All right." Niki fell back, bracing herself with her arms. Immediately he began flicking his tongue back and forth against her nipple, bringing it to rigid alertness.

"I never tasted anything so good," he said around her flesh. "I can't get enough of you, Niki."

He nipped lightly, then sucked the tingling tip deep into his mouth. Convulsions started in the pit of her belly and increased as he sucked with increasing intensity.

Her last coherent thought before he blew her away for the second time was that this could easily get to be a habit.

THEY FINALLY made the passage from kitchen to bedroom, but it took a while because they stopped to kiss and caress and play whenever the spirit moved them, which was frequently. If the kitchen was a sexy explosion, the bedroom was a sensual exploration.

They made love and they talked. "I want to know what you didn't tell me the other time," he said, holding her, totally exhausted but also totally gratified, in his arms.

She kissed his flat nipple, enjoying the tremor which ran through him. "About what?"

"You and your mother. How you're alike in more than looks...."

She sighed. "I should never have mentioned that. It's not something I'm proud of."

"There are a few things I'm not entirely proud of, either," he said, suddenly serious. "You tell me yours and I'll tell you mine."

That dragged a laugh out of her. "I thought that was '*show* me yours,' etcetera."

"Whatever. The point is, I want to know everything there is to know about you."

She made a conscious decision to trust him then. "Please don't repeat this, Clay. My family doesn't even know the details." Faintly lit by moonlight streaming through the windows, she chewed on her lower lip, then said, "Like my mother, I fell for an unsuitable man when I was young and foolish. He was more than twenty years older and light-years more sophisticated."

"How old were you?"

"Seventeen. I..." She peered at him closely, as if looking for assurance that she wasn't making a fool out of herself. He hoped he gave her that. "I got pregnant," she said flatly, "also like my mother."

He couldn't believe what he'd just heard. "You had a *baby?*"

Her head rolled from side to side on his arm. "I had a miscarriage so early that no one else knew about it but me."

"The man?" He held a cold fury at bay.

"Left town the minute I even suspected—and I was glad." For the first time, she sounded bitter. "He only wanted me because I was pretty and a challenge. At least, I suppose a seventeen-year-old virgin was a challenge ten years ago." Dark lashes fluttered down. "I guess it could have been worse. I learned my lesson without being tied to a good-for-nothing—" She bit off her words.

"Go on," he said gently, stroking her, trying to soothe her. "Get it all off your chest, honey."

"The rest is obvious. My father wasn't interested in kids and certainly not in three of them at a time. After he left, that was it—he never sent mother a penny and he never showed the slightest interest in us. We grew up not knowing if he was dead or alive and not caring much, either. Then about three years ago, we inherited this place from him out of the blue. I guess he thought he could make up for not being around or something. More likely, he didn't have anyone else to leave it to."

"Or maybe he was alone and sorry about what he'd done," Clay suggested gently. "I don't want to offend you, but he sounds like a pretty pathetic case to me."

"I suppose." She let out her breath slowly, feeling surprisingly better.

"One more thing…"

"Ummm?"

"The scar on the back of your knee…?"

"It's nothing," she said quickly. "Okay, now it's your turn. You tell me yours."

"Not nearly as interesting. My folks died together in a car crash in California when I was ten. I was sent to live on a ranch in Oklahoma with an aunt and uncle who didn't have any kids, didn't want any kids, and didn't like kids anyway. I started running away when I was eleven. When I was seventeen, they stopped looking for me. Today we're civil, but little more. Funny thing is, I'm their only heir and like you, I'll probably get the whole enchilada someday. Like I care."

"Oh!" She snuggled against him. "That's tough. At least I grew up with lots of love—from Mother until she died, but always from my sisters and Grandma."

"Yeah." He nuzzled her hair. "Guess I've been lookin' for love in all the wrong places ever since."

And then a brand new idea struck him like a bolt of lightning: maybe at last he was looking for love in the *right* place. Because nothing had ever felt more right than holding this woman in his arms, talking to her, making love to her.

She smothered a yawn. "I haven't been looking for love at all." She pounded a fist lightly on his shoulder. "Until you came along, Clay Russell." Her chuckle was low and intimate. "Considering where we are, I'm going to assume you've made your choice."

"What choice?" he asked cautiously.

"The choice I gave you—between me, the celebrity cowgirl, and me in your bed. Remember that one? Under the circumstances, I think we can dispense with any further hassle about that darned cowgirl contest."

That's what she thinks, he told himself, holding her drowsy body close. He didn't want one or the other of those things, he wanted both.

Now more than ever.

GRANNY was in the kitchen banging away with pots and pans by five o'clock the next morning. Niki knew because the clatter woke her up hours before she wanted to face the world.

She was exhausted. And stiff—she climbed out of bed groaning and looked down at Clay, sleeping as peacefully as a baby. What a night they'd had! Nothing would ever be the same again, for now she knew things she hadn't known before.

Such as the power of sex—raw, unadorned sex. Tender sex, gentle sex, sex with a man who made her heart bang wildly in her breast and form questions she wasn't able to answer.

Such as, what did he really think of her? Had he made love to her just to get her to change her mind about the competition? Because she was wavering, heaven help her. The thought of spending the next year traveling around the country with him... making love to him every night—

A shower, maybe even a cold shower, was what she needed. But first she had to get him out of her bed before Granny took a notion to come upstairs. Leaning over, she gripped his shoulder and gave him a shake.

"Clay! Wake up. You've got to get out of here. Granny's downstairs and—"

"Huh?" Grabbing her, he rolled her over onto her back and rolled himself on top of her. Eyes still

closed, he nuzzled her cheek and tried to slide his
knee between her thighs.

"Clay!" She struggled to escape, trying not to
laugh. "This is no time for hanky-panky! You've got
to get out of here!"

He reared back, finally opening one eye to squint
at her. Golden-brown hair spilled over his forehead,
giving him a roguish air. "It's always a good time for
hanky-panky."

"Spoken like a *man*." She finally managed to
scramble away from him and sit up.

"I *am* a man," he said reasonably, a lazy grin curving his mouth. "that's why I talk like one, probably."
But he was starting to wake up, at last. "Have you
forgotten so soon?"

"Not hardly." She have him a rueful smile over a
bare shoulder. Grabbing her robe off the floor, she
stood and pulled it on in one motion. "I've got to get
myself together and go downstairs to help Granny
with breakfast. You can sleep in your *own* room,
buster."

He sat up, the sheet pooling around his hips. He
was beautiful: broad shouldered and well-muscled.

And scarred.

She frowned. "What's happened to you?" She
leaned forward to examine the criss-crossing of
white lines on his torso. "How did you—?"

"Sorry, the lady says I gotta get out of here." Leaping up in all his naked glory, he looked around. "Where's my towel?"

She gasped. "Downstairs in the kitchen with my T-shirt. Oh, no—!"

What a way to start the day!

GRANDMA didn't seem to think anything about finding an oversize T-shirt and a damp towel on the kitchen floor. She never even mentioned it when Niki bustled in to help, nor later when she casually picked up the items and deposited them in the laundry basket on the screened-in back porch.

Granny noticed something else, though. She paused in the act of flipping pancakes on a griddle and announced, "Niki dear, you look exhausted this morning. Are you coming down with something?"

Mortified, Niki hoped her face wasn't as red as it felt. "I'm f-fine," she stammered. "I...just didn't sleep very well last night."

"You take it easy today, then." Grandma nodded for emphasis. "I think these pancakes are just about ready if you want to carry them into the dining room."

Niki did, and the first person she saw was Clay, standing near the coffee service while speaking to an enthralled circle of dudes. He didn't look exhausted, he looked just fine...wonderful, in fact. He looked up, saw her and winked.

She gave an indignant sniff and turned away to

put the pancakes in the warming tray. This day was not starting out to be one of her best.

Guess that's what a guilty conscience did to a person.

NIKI HAD JUST FINISHED vacuuming the Great Room at mid-morning when the front door opened and a stranger walked in. And what a stranger!

Tall, sleek and impeccably dressed in a pink suit that fit like a leotard, she smiled as she came forward with an outstretched hand. The closer she got, the more impressed Niki was. Looking somewhere between forty-five and sixty, the woman wore her blond hair in a sleek French twist. Her makeup was not subtle, but so perfectly applied that Niki could only stare in awe.

Sophistication simply *oozed* from this woman when she stretched out her hand and said, "Hello, Niki. I'm Eve Hubbard."

At that point, the bottom *really* dropped out of Niki's world.

8

"Ms. Hubbard!" Niki accepted the proffered hand, wondering what on earth this unexpected visit might mean. "We weren't expecting you. Clay didn't say anything about you dropping by."

"He didn't know, dear girl." The woman looked around at the overly western room, her expression faintly ironic. "And please call me Eve." Suddenly all business, she returned her attention to the dumfounded Niki. "You're the reason I'm here, of course."

Niki's jaw tightened. "Then I'm afraid you've wasted the trip."

"I never waste anything." Eve looked the younger woman over, her heavily mascaraed eyes narrowing to mere slits of calculation. "That's a Mother Hubbard original you're wearing there."

Niki glanced down in surprise. She didn't even remember what she'd put on this morning, she'd been so agitated. But she wasn't surprised to find herself in lavender jeans with fringe up the side seams and a matching T-shirt. "You're right," she admitted. "I wear a lot of Wild West Duds, actually. They're comfortable and I like the way they look."

"I like the way they look on *you*."

"Thank you, I guess." Niki bit her lower lip, still wondering what the point of this visit might be. "Uhh...Clay must have told you that I'm going to withdraw from your contest."

"He mentioned something along those lines, but I disregarded it."

"No, I mean it, and he's agreed not to badger me about it any longer. In fact, I wouldn't be surprised if he's thinking about leaving himself, now that he sees there's no further hope I'll change my mind." Regret pierced her heart when she said it. His departure could very well be the result of what had happened between them last night. She'd given him a choice, more or less: the lady or the contest. He'd taken the lady, but it was strictly a one-shot deal.

That meant he no longer had an excuse to hang around the ranch trying to get her to reconsider. Once he left, her life would return to normal.

Maybe.

Eve still looked dubious. "This is very strange," she announced, "since this contest is as important to him as it is to the winner."

"How so?" Niki couldn't help asking.

"Because without a suitable Queen of the Cowgirls, his part in our advertising thrust has just about run its course. Whereas with an appropriate queen, he'll have a whole new lease on life as company spokesman."

"I can't believe it would be a tragedy if he simply returned to his own business," Niki said. "After all, he's really a rodeo star, not a model or spokesman."

"Was."

"Was?"

"A rodeo star. After that latest injury, it's beginning to look as if he won't be able to do that any longer."

"I don't understand." Niki frowned at the woman. "What latest injury?"

"The one he got here, dear. But not to worry. Mother Hubbard will keep him on for at least two more years, maybe more, if a suitable Queen of the Cowgirls is forthcoming. Why, that could even lead to an acting career!"

Niki's head reeled. "He wants to be an actor?" she asked faintly.

"Who doesn't?" Eve shrugged off all doubt. "So as far as being resigned to your withdrawal, I hate to burst your bubble, but he isn't. No more than I am. Just this morning he left a message on my machine saying, and I quote, 'The situation is looking up.' Does that sound like a resigned man?"

"N-no."

"Exactly. Well." Eve straightened. "If you'll show me to my room, I'll get settled in."

Niki gasped. "You intend to stay *here?*"

"Of course."

"But that's impossible!"

Eve's eyes narrowed. "I didn't drive all the way from Dallas just to say hello."

"But...but we're all full up. I don't have anyplace to put you."

"In Clay's room, if necessary—now, don't look so shocked." Eve laughed heartily. "He can sleep somewhere else—in the barn, whatever. He's tough. He won't mind."

"All the cabins are full. Clay's sleeping here in the house."

"Excellent." Eve waited expectantly.

"I suppose I could put you in Toni's room."

"I'd really prefer to inconvenience someone I know as opposed to a total stranger."

Niki's smile eased her tension. "Toni's my sister. She got married a while back so her room's empty."

"Then what's the problem?" Eve spread her arms in a questioning gesture.

"No problem. It's just that we try to keep the house for family."

"Think of *me* as family," Eve suggested. "Now if you'll excuse me, I'll grab my bag and you can show me where I go."

Niki nodded, but her thoughts were tumbling. So Clay *had* been using sex to manipulate her for his own gains. Talk about having your cake and eating it, too! Doubtless he believed that a night in his arms would be so glorious that it would soften her up for *anything*. Okay, it had been glorious, she couldn't deny that, but Eve's revelations had just reinforced her determination not to change her mind about the contest.

The door swung open and Eve walked inside, empty-handed, but with sparkling eyes. Turning, she held the door wide.

Travis Burke entered beaming. Sun-browned and mustached, Travis was the picture of a true Man of the West—the Marlboro man without the cigarette. Many-times married and divorced, he'd sworn off women, according to his daughter-in-law, Dani.

Seeing him now, you sure wouldn't have known it. He was looking at Eve like a cat looks at cream.

Eve smiled at Niki. "This gentleman offered to carry my bag and knowing a good thing when I see it, I let him. He says you'll vouch for him."

"I sure will. How's it going, Travis?"

"Fine. Just fine." He handled Eve's small leather bag with ease. "Dani sent me over to pick up some stuff from Grandma."

"Who's Dani?" Eve inquired, looking interested.

"She's married to my son, Jack," Travis said. "She's also Niki's sister—triplet, actually."

"You mean there's *three* of you?" Eve asked Niki with delight.

Niki grinned. "Sort of. We're triplets, but we're not identical, if that's what you're thinking."

Eve's brows rose. "Too much of a good thing is wonderful," she declared, "but I'll settle for one."

"You'll settle for none if you're talking about—"

"*Eve?* Good God, what are *you* doing here?" Clay, entering from the dining room, sounded—and looked—incredulous.

"I came to see—"

The front door opened to admit Granny. "My goodness," she said, "I see we have company."

While Travis did the honors, Niki stole a glance at Clay. Apparently Eve's appearance was a bigger shock to him that it had been to Niki.

As if he had something to hide, actually. Deliberately she turned away from him.

"Ms. Hubbard, your room—"

"Later, dear." Eve linked her arm with Travis's as if they were old friends...old lovers...old somethings. "Your darling grandmother mentioned tea and I could certainly do with a cup after that long drive."

"I'll join you," Travis said alertly—Travis, who occasionally dropped into the Sorry Bastard for a beer and a chance to scoff at those who chose anything lighter.

Grandma's head bobbed approvingly. "Will you join us, dear? You, too, Clay."

Clay glanced at Niki, obviously waiting for her response.

Which came in the form of a negative shake of the head. "I have too much to do."

"Anything I can help you with?" Clay asked quickly.

"No. Thanks anyway." She turned away.

"Niki—"

She turned back, a polite smile plastered on her face, just in time to see the other three disappear into the dining room. "Yes?"

"Don't be this way." He moved toward her. "I didn't know Eve was coming."

"I believe you."

"Then what's got you all worked up?"

"Gee, I don't know. Do you suppose it could be the message you left on her machine this morning?"

"What message?"

"The message that said, 'the situation is looking up?'" She resisted the desire to grit her teeth. "Well, the situation for getting me to change my mind is *not* looking up!"

"How do you know that's what I meant?"

"It's what *she* thought you meant."

"Eve tends to interpret everything to suit her own purposes. What I really meant was—"

"Spare me the explanations. I know what you really meant. Now if you'll excuse me, I do have work to do."

Back straight, she marched up the stairs and into

her room, at which point she collapsed against her door in despair.

WHEN NIKI WALKED into the kitchen a half hour later, the tea party was still going strong. Clay was nowhere in sight; probably leading the morning trail ride. Lunch would be waiting when they returned and then there was the evening meal to contend with as well.

Trying to be diplomatic, she cleared her throat. "What should I do first, Granny?"

"Sheila's already made the salads and lunch is a casserole ready to pop into the oven." Granny turned to Eve. "Tonight's the big steak fry and hoedown," she confided. "I expect you'll get a big kick out of it."

"I'm sure I will," Eve agreed. She glanced at Travis, sitting entranced at her side. "You'll be there, of course."

Since Travis looked tongue-tied, Niki tried to give him an out. "Travis has his own dude ranch, the XOX, and that keeps him pretty busy."

"Oh, piffle!" Eve brushed aside the biggest ranch in the Hill Country. "Of *course* he'll come...for me. Won't you, Travis."

"For you..." Travis looked downright mesmerized. "Heck, yeah. You can count on me."

"Excellent." Eve rose. "On that happy thought, I think it's time to let this child show me to my room. Until tonight, Travis."

"Oh, yeah."

Niki led Eve from the room, hiding her smile. Just wait until Dani heard about this!

THE MUSIC was lively, but at least one pair of dancers weren't.

Pausing in the act of removing dishes from the long picnic table, Niki looked at Eve and Travis with amazement. She'd never seen such a fast and furious flirtation as the one unfolding before her.

"They're quite a couple."

Clay's voice in her ear, unanticipated as always, made her start. She was almost getting used to being ambushed this way. Shrugging, she continued stacking dishes.

But they *were* quite a couple, the handsome and rugged rancher and the blond sophisticate in a white linen suit. Talk about a romance doomed to go nowhere.

Clay scooted a couple of glasses forward to be added to her plastic tub. "You've been avoiding me," he said.

"You know why."

"No, I don't." He cocked his head. "You're not still mad about that telephone call."

"Among other things." Hoisting the tub, she turned away.

He stopped her, took the tub from her hands. "You've got to talk to me, Niki."

"Actually, I don't. I don't think there's anything to be gained by more talk. We both know exactly how things are and we're never going to agree on how they should be, so why get into it again?"

"Perhaps in the spirit of compromise," he suggested, glancing around impatiently. "Isn't there somewhere around here where we can have a little privacy?"

"Privacy is the last thing I want. If you're not going to let me have those dishes, then you'd better take them back to the kitchen. I need to check the drink table so if you'll excuse me..."

She wound through the crowd, smiling automatically at those she met or passed. The wooden platform used for dancing and impromptu shows was comfortably full of couples. With the three-piece band performing at one end, no one showed any inclination to end the party early.

Except Niki, but first she had to tidy up the drink table and make sure the cooler contained sufficient beverages. Off to one side, she saw Granny reading the riot act to old Dobe Whittaker; on the other, Eve and Travis swung into a dreamy dance with her head on his shoulder. Lights twinkled in the trees overhead and a bright sliver of moon beamed down romantically.

And here stood Niki, more alone than she'd been before she ever laid eyes on one Clay Russell. She sighed.

Dylan, in the act of tossing a paper cup into the trash receptacle, noticed. "What's the matter, Nik? You don't look much in a party mood."

"You noticed." She dredged up a smile and tried to speak lightly.

"C'mon, then." He wiggled his fingers and grinned. "Let's take us a little spin around the dance floor and see if maybe that'll cheer you up."

"Oh, I doubt—" But then she saw Clay making his way toward her, his expression determined, and she changed her mind. "Why not?" She took Dylan's hand. "Show me some fancy stuff, cowboy."

So went the rest of the evening.

MOST OF THE GUESTS had wandered back to their cabins. Niki only had one more trip to finish clearing the party area while Granny put things away in the kitchen. What had happened to Clay, Niki didn't know, but she was grateful for his absence.

It had been a difficult evening, trying to avoid him and any further phony protestations of innocence. She didn't believe a word he said and never would, so talking was futile.

Even more so now that they'd been intimate. She closed her eyes tightly, trying to erase those memories. Was it just last night that they'd fallen into each other's arms? Sexual attraction was a mysterious thing. Why was she so attracted to this man? He was handsome but so what? A lot of handsome men had fallen at her feet. He was charming and talented, but that was another big "So what?"

Chalk it up to experience and move on, she thought tiredly. Opening her eyes, she blinked at Eve, peering at her quizzically with Travis right behind her.

"Are you with us again, Niki?"

Niki gave an embarrassed laugh. "Sorry to zone out that way. What can I do for you?"

"Give me a house key."

"A what?"

Eve laughed. "This is like living in a dorm and having to justify being out late. I'm going over to Travis's to see his etchings."

Travis let out a choked little exclamation and she laughed again. "What's the matter, do they call it something else these days? The truth is, I'm very likely going to let this man have his way with me but I need a key so I can get back into the house after lockdown."

Thunderstruck by the woman's frankness, Niki concentrated on Travis, who looked positively mortified. He did not, however, protest.

"You can grab a key from the hook beside the desk in the Great Room," she said. "Y'all have a good time."

Eve squeezed Travis's arm. "We intend to. Good night to you, too."

Turning, they walked arm in arm to the front door

and up the steps to disappear inside. Taking a deep breath, Niki sat down on a picnic bench and stared up into the sky, past twinkling lights to twinkling stars. A feeling of vast loneliness swept over her and she shivered, despite the muggy Texas air.

Clay had done this to her. She'd never been lonely in her life until he barged in and made her want things she thought she'd put behind her...things like men and sex and love forever after. She'd been weakened by her sisters' happiness, she supposed; by their delight in their husbands and the birth of Elsie. Clay had appeared when she was at her most vulnerable, that was all.

But now that she understood how dangerous he was, he wouldn't get a chance to lead her down the garden path again.

Not again, not even after she watched Travis and Eve walk hand in hand to his pickup truck and drive away, leaving Eve's car alone and lonely in the parking lot.

Men.

Picking up a tray of condiments, Niki stomped off to the kitchen.

"Niki—Niki, let me in." The soft impact of a hand flat on the bedroom door accompanied Clay's plea.

In the act of turning down her bed, Niki froze. Her alarmed gaze centered on the door, visualizing the man behind it as he'd been last night. She straightened, pulling down her T-shirt self-consciously. She wouldn't let him in tonight—she wouldn't!

"Niki! I know you're in there. I'm not going away until you talk to me."

He spoke softly, but Granny was sleeping just down the hall. Despite herself, Niki flew to the door and pressed herself flat against it.

"Stop it, Clay. Go away. You'll wake up the household."

"If I do, it'll be your fault." Another pat on the door, this one heavier. "Are you going to let me in or do I have to—"

Without pausing to let herself be dissuaded by cold reason, Niki threw wide the door. "Will you stop?" she hissed. "Say what you have to say and let me go to bed."

"I can't say it standing in the hall." Lifting her by stiff elbows, he set her aside, walked in and closed the door behind him.

He wore jeans, nothing more: no shirt, no shoes. His lean brown torso tapered down to a narrow waist and by lamplight, she once again saw several wicked scars bisecting his ribs on the right side. She caught her breath, remembering what Eve had said about his poor prospects for returning to rodeo.

He was looking at her, too, his gaze growing progressively hotter. She took several quick steps back and said, "Say what you have to say and go away."

"I...apologize."

"For...?"

"Anything and everything." He shrugged help-lessly and took a step toward her, his arms opening and his expression appealing.

"You mean you don't *know* what you're apologiz-ing for?" She gritted her teeth in frustration. "Clay, I told you it was me or that damned contest and you obviously took me—"

"Oh, yeah, that."

"—so the next morning you call Eve and tell her everything's looking *up?*"

"I told you I wanted both. I didn't know I was making a deal."

He picked up one of her cold hands and held it be-tween both of his warm ones and she didn't even have the self-possession to pull away. This close to him, all her good intentions seemed to fly right out of her head.

"Niki," he went on earnestly, "when I called Eve I was flying. I'd just spent a fantastic night with a woman who has intrigued and perplexed me ever since I met her. Things were looking up with *you*, on a personal level anyway."

She stiffened. "Then tell me right here and now that you have given up all hope that I'll participate in that glorified publicity stunt."

For a long moment he just stood there. Then he said sadly, "I can't do that. Of *course* I hope you'll change your mind. I want to spend the next year or two with *you* and not some wanna-be model or actress. I want time to get to know you, really know you. I want you to know me." He looked intensely frustrated. "So sue me."

"Oh, *Clay...*"

His name on her lips ended in a groan. When he stepped close, she didn't pull back because she simply couldn't. When he slipped his arms around her, she melted against him, lifting her face eagerly to accept his kiss.

Because now she knew what it was like to be loved by this man...or at least, to have this man make love to her. A subtle yet important distinction, which she couldn't hang on to because his tongue teased her mouth, then slipped inside, while his eager hands fondled her breasts. In a flash, he'd deftly awakened the craving she'd confronted only the night before.

She felt starved for him, despite the fact that he'd left her sated only twenty-four hours earlier. His hands on her breasts sent a newly-familiar hot excitement flooding through her to puddle at the pit of her stomach.

She was hot and wet and ready for him, and humiliated to realize it. As he had the night before, he swept the T-shirt over her head, deftly removing her only defense. Naked in the subdued lighting of the room, she let him look his fill.

"You're so beautiful." The same words she'd always heard, but not said in awe this time, more in exultation. "I wanted to see you last night but everything happened at warp speed."

"So now you've seen me." Her voice came out strangled and rough because she'd heard it all before. "If you didn't like what you saw, would you leave?"

"Leave?" His head flew back and he stared at her with burning eyes. "What's your point?

"That I get so sick of being held up to some impossible standard of what I should look like and act like and be." She lifted her breasts with her hands, glaring at him. "My breasts don't sag and my waist is small and my legs are long. Is that all it takes?"

He laughed, his white teeth flashing. "No, but that's a helluva start. I see I've aggravated you by admiring you so I'm gonna let you get even by admiring me." With a quick motion, he unsnapped his waistband and shoved down his jeans. He wore nothing underneath.

With a broad smile he faced her, buck naked, arms stretched wide. "Take me," he commanded. "I'm yours."

AND SHE DID, to his astonished pleasure. In her bed, she pressed him onto his back and rolled over him, her warm thigh sliding between his legs. Her hands moved over him like wildfire, her warm mouth following until he trembled beneath the sensual onslaught.

Then she rose above him...straddled his hips and lowered herself slowly and deliberately over the hard length of him. Her actions tore a groan from his throat. Firmly seated, she leaned forward, that long thick black hair brushing his face, his chest.

She began to move...slowly and deliberately at first, then picking up the pace. Her eyes closed, the long black lashes lacy across the most incredible cheekbones in the western world. Grasping her hips, he adjusted her movements to match his. He could feel her contractions begin, squeezing him...spurring him....

A muffled cry—her eyes flew open, deep purple with passion. She looked stunned with the force of her orgasm and he was just behind her, unable to bear it another second. With reckless abandon he thrust into her and surrendered to convulsive tremors. Shocked and thrilled, he let himself go with it. Even in the throes of passion, he slid his arms around her in a possessive embrace that took her with him.

SHE STILL LAY GASPING on top of him when she heard the front door open downstairs. Immediately she stiffened and tried to roll away.

He wouldn't let her go. "Not so fast," he mumbled in a sleepy voice. "Let's just lay here for a minute and—"

"No time for that." She pushed out of his arms. "Eve's home."

"So?" He tried to pull her back into his embrace.

"So I don't want her to know what's going on. She—" Niki bit her quivering lower lip. "She'd get the wrong idea."

"I doubt it." He rubbed one hand down her spine. Her skin felt silky smooth and so very alive. "Niki, have I told you lately that you're—"

"If you say 'beautiful,' I swear I'll call the cops!"

He frowned. "I was going to say—To hell with it, you wouldn't believe me anyway."

He sounded so affronted that she immediately felt ashamed of herself. "Go ahead, I want to hear."

"I was going to say you're a helluva lay." He sat up and slid his legs over the edge of the bed. "Does that satisfy you?"

"Not particularly."

"Okay, try this." Rising, he crossed the room to pick up his jeans. "I was going to say you're a helluva woman. Better?"

"Maybe." He was confusing her. Which of those things represented his true feelings?

"How about—"

"That's enough," she said sharply. Sitting, she pulled the chenille bedspread over her breasts and beneath her arms. "Just go."

"Now? For all we know, she's right outside this door."

"I don't care! Just go!"

He went. She stared at the closed door for a moment, wishing him back, wishing him gone, wishing...

Dropping back onto the pillows, she stared up at the ceiling, thinking that just once she'd like someone to tell her she was smart. No, that was Dani. Or nice, but of course, that was Toni. Experience had made her leery of men who'd use her for her beauty and Clay was the worst of the lot because he'd made her fall for him in the process.

Fall hard. With soft frustration, she pounded a fist on the bed at her side and muttered, "Damn, damn and double damn!"

CLAY STEPPED into the hall and almost bumped into Eve, standing there looking at him with that quizzical expression which always drove him crazy. Before he could speak, she put her fingers to her lips and gestured him down the hall.

He went because he didn't want Niki to know. He understood instinctively that she'd be humiliated to be found out this way.

Eve opened the door to her room and gestured him inside, then followed, closing the door behind them.

"Well, well, well," she purred. "I knew you were a loyal employee, but this is—"

"Don't go there, Eve." The words exploded out of him. He wasn't going to stand here and listen to her belittle something that he suddenly realized meant a hell of a lot to him.

Her eyes widened. "Sorry, I didn't mean to offend anybody. Believe me, this pot isn't going to call the kettle names." She dropped her clutch purse onto the desk against the wall.

"Okay, let's forget the whole thing."

"Not so fast."

"Eve..." But where could he go with this? Even though she'd caught him coming out of Niki's room barely dressed, he wasn't prepared to confirm her suspicions. On the other hand, since she obviously knew he hadn't been in there playing tic-tac-toe, maybe he should make it clear that what he'd done had been personal, not for the good of Mother Hubbard.

To hell with that. "Look," he said, "I'm tired and I'm going to bed. Think what you want, but if you believe I've just given my all for Mother Hubbard, you've got the wrong boy. Loyalty is one thing, but I've gotta draw the line somewhere. What kind of a lowlife do you think I am?"

He walked out the door. She didn't try to stop him, for which he was grateful because he didn't *want* to know how stupid she thought he was.

He had to admit that making love to Niki Keene sure as hell made him feel stupid—stupid because the bliss of the moment always seemed to make him forget all the problems and difficulties they still faced.

He was going to have to do something about that...but what?

9

EVERYBODY LOVED Eve Hubbard.

By the time Niki finished breakfast preparations and took her seat, Eve had the entire dining room enthralled.

"...and then I said, I only design 'em, I don't wear 'em. I can't do my own clothes justice. That's why I hire sweet young things to carry my message." Her laserlike eyes burned into Niki. "Like Niki Keene, over there in the corner trying to look inconspicuous. Is she Queen of the Cowgirls material or is she not?"

Applause burst out spontaneously as all the dudes responded to the appeal. That was Eve, working the room.

Clay didn't show up for breakfast. Anxious, Niki drifted out to the corral later to make sure he was there for the morning trail ride. He was, so she drifted away again, striving to remain inconspicuous.

She'd just started straightening the Great Room after lunch when Eve entered, leather suitcase in hand. As usual, she looked perfectly groomed and put together in a turquoise silk suit. Not as usual, she was frowning.

"Have you heard anything from Travis Burke today?" she demanded.

"No. Was he supposed to call?"

The frown deepened. "One of us was," Eve said darkly. "Anyway, I've come to say goodbye."

"You're leaving?" Niki felt both relief and disappointment at the news. Eve was entertaining, if nothing else.

"Duty calls." Eve spoke lightly but there seemed to be some effort behind it. "Before I go, I've got to make one more pitch for you to stay in my contest."

"Thank you, no."

"Even if we put it on a personal level? You'd do it for *me*, wouldn't you, Niki?"

Niki couldn't believe the woman's gall and burst out laughing. "I don't even *know* you. Why would I do it for you when I won't do it for my grandmother or my sisters or the entire town?"

"Because you like me?" Eve's smile turned winsome. "Hell, it was worth a shot." She gripped her suitcase handle more tightly. "You haven't heard the last of this, dear heart."

"Oh, puh-*leeze* let this be the last of it!" Niki rose and followed her to the door. Clay loitered near Eve's sports car and her heart skipped a beat.

"You should listen to Mother Hubbard," Eve said

sternly. She winked. "Whatever. I'm sure we'll see each other soon."

Not until after that blasted contest is over, Niki prayed. But what she said was, "Perhaps. Drive carefully." Closing the door, she told herself she'd prefer to keep Eve and send Clay away.

Sure she would.

EVE SLAMMED her case into the trunk of the Porsche and glared at Clay. "Go ahead," she invited. "Kick me while I'm down."

"I'm not kickin' anyone," he said. "I just came to say goodbye."

"Goodbye." She opened the car door. "If that's all..."

"Dammit, it's not all." Frustrated, he kicked at a weed. "I didn't handle last night real well, when I ran into you in the hall, I mean."

"I know what you mean and you're right. You *didn't* handle it real well."

"Yeah, well, it's just that my relationship with Niki is nobody's business but ours."

"Fine. So let's talk professionally." She jabbed a stiff forefinger into his chest. "Either Niki's my Queen of Cowgirls or I'm going to dump the current campaign entirely and go back to the little old white-haired lady. That means you, my boy, will be out on the street."

That prediction made his gut clench. He'd been on

the street and didn't like it a helluva lot. But he chose bravado, nonetheless. "You're not exaggerating just a little bit, are you?"

"I believe I'm telling it like it is." She spoke with chilling conviction. "I like you, Clay, but business is business. We've gone as far as we can with the rodeo-champ gambit. If Niki comes on board, that would prolong your usefulness."

Of all the unreasonable... "Jeez, Eve, there are eleven other women in this contest," he reminded her.

"Do *you* think any of them compare with Niki?"

"No, but I—" He stopped short, appalled, wondering what the hell he thought he was about to say: *No, but I...know Niki, slept with Niki, love—*

When he didn't go on, Eve did. "I never settle for second best," she said coolly. "Which means you have your work cut out for you because the competition is one week from today. Don't let either one of us down."

She climbed into the car, started the engine, lowered the window and leaned out, her eyes icy cold. "And if you see that son of a bitch, Travis Burke, you can tell him for me—"

The rest was thankfully lost in the roar of the engine, the peal of rubber and the spray of gravel and dust. But Clay could guess what she'd been about to say. All he didn't know was why.

TRAVIS GALLOPED into the ranch yard not fifteen minutes later on a lathered horse. He stepped out of the saddle before the animal could come to a full stop and took the ranch house steps two at a time and slammed inside.

Niki, crossing the lawn from the pool on her way back to the main house, picked up speed, careful to avoid the heaving horse tied to the front rail. Travis himself had looked fit to be tied and the horse looked even worse.

The front door flew open and Travis burst out onto the porch, Clay right behind him.

"Where is she?" Travis demanded, looking around wildly. "Son of a— I got here as soon as I could, but it looks like I'm too late."

"If 'she' is Eve Hubbard, you just missed her." Niki put her hands on her hips and peered up at him. "What's going on, Travis?"

"Ah, it's all a misunderstanding." He stomped down the steps. "Did she leave me a message?"

"No. She asked if you'd called, that's all."

"Damn!" He looked around helplessly, as if he thought this was all a bad joke and Eve would jump out yelling *Surprise!* "My damn pickup had a damn flat and there was no time to change it. We must have fifteen vehicles on the XOX and do you think I could find one when I needed it?"

Clay laughed. "So you jumped on a horse?"

"It was that or walk," Travis flared.

"Well, you missed her," Niki said. He looked so distraught that she was starting to feel sorry for him. "Why don't you come inside and have a nice glass of lemonade? It'll make you feel better."

"I doubt it."

"I can give you her Dallas number," Clay offered. "Or her cell phone."

"Forget it." Travis threw back his shoulders defiantly and his eyes narrowed. "She could have waited if it meant anything to her. Or she could have driven over to the XOX." He shrugged. "To hell with that. I'm goin' home."

He walked to his horse, grabbed the saddle horn and swung up, every inch the western hero. If Eve could have seen him at that moment, Niki thought, she'd be putty in his hands.

Brooding over the injustices of life, she turned back to the steps—and Clay standing at the top of them, waiting for her with a thoughtful expression on his face. Teeth clenched, she waited for him to speak.

He did. "Time's getting short," he said.

For what? For them? Her heart lurched painfully but she stood her ground. "And your point is...?"

"It's finally dawning on me that this go-round, I may not get my way."

"About...?"

"The contest, what else?" He said irritably. "All

the contestants are due at Eve's ranch outside Dallas a week from yesterday."

"I wish them luck." She walked up the steps past him and entered the house.

He followed. "There's still time, Niki. Dammit, don't walk away from me like that!" Catching her by the upper arm, he swung her around to face him. "I think I've got to know you a little these past few weeks and for the life of me, I don't know what's holding you back except pure stubbornness."

She didn't try to pull away, just glared back at him. Anger was the only defense she had. "It's more than that."

"No, it isn't. You're not some little shrinking violet who gets nervous when people look at you. And I sure as hell don't believe the thought of spending the next year or two with me is all that revolting to you."

"I don't have to explain myself to you," she said, tight-lipped.

But he was on a roll. "So that only leaves..." His dark eyes widened. "Is it your fear of horses?"

"Certainly not." Now she did yank free. "Maybe. I mean, really, can you imagine the problems it would create to have a Queen of the Cowgirls who's afraid of horses?"

"You can get over that."

"I don't *want* to get over that." She whirled and headed for the kitchen, head down. She was ashamed of her fear of horses, but she'd lived with it for so long that the thought of confronting it nearly paralyzed her with dread.

"I can help you." Clay kept pace with her easily. "You just got off to a bad start, that's all. There's a nice little paint mare in the herd who'd be perfect for—"

"*No!*" Driven beyond endurance, she faced him. "Which part of 'I want nothing to do with horses' don't you understand? Please don't mention this to me again."

"But—"

"Clay, I mean it. Now if you'll excuse me, I'm due at the Sorry Bastard in forty-five minutes."

He heard her footsteps on the stair, but his thoughts were elsewhere. It didn't take much to sit on top of a fat, lazy trail horse ambling along. Hell, dudes did it every day. If he could just get her to give riding one more chance.

The way things stood now, he'd have to drag her to it kicking and screaming. Unless...

Nah, he couldn't take a chance like that...could he?

Eve called Clay two days later. "Any luck?" she demanded bluntly.

"Nope." It pained him to admit it but he wouldn't prevaricate.

An audible sigh passed over the telephone wire. "In that case, I'm officially informing you that no Niki, no Clay."

His gut clenched. "What, you mean you're hiring a hit man?"

"Very funny. I mean that the current ad campaign will end and with it, our need for your services as spokesman."

Clay gritted his teeth and said nothing. What was there to say?

The truth was, if Niki wasn't the Queen of Cowgirls he didn't want to do the new campaign anyway. Even though he'd need the money if he never went back to rodeo...

"Well? Did you hear what I said?"

"I heard, Eve."

"Don't you have anything to say?"

"Yep."

"Then say it!"

"If Niki doesn't change her mind, it'll hurt me more than it does you."

"I thought you'd see the light." Eve's voice dropped to a satisfied purr. "We'll survive. We'll just go on to another advertising campaign. On the other hand, you need the income."

Not nearly as much as he needed Niki. Niki, who'd taken to barricading her bedroom door. Niki, who could make him crazy with a glance. Niki, who—

"I hate it when you get all quiet on me," she said. "You haven't given up, have you?"

"I haven't given up." Although he knew he probably should.

"Good. Do your best. Tell her I'm willing to negotiate the contract over and above the contest prizes."

"If she does this, it won't be for the prizes."

"Then what the hell would it be for? Whatever it is, give it to her!" Eve laughed ruefully. "Whatever. All we can do is all we can do."

"Right. If that's all..."

"Not quite," she said sharply. "Did...uh...do you see much of Travis since I left?"

"Not much."

"Did he...ask for my phone numbers or...or anything? Because if he did, you have my permission to give them to him."

Well, hell. Now he was either going to have to lie or tell her the truth and hurt her feelings: that he'd offered the numbers and been turned down. "I got a better idea," he said. "I can give you the number at the XOX and you can call *him*."

"Me, call him? Not a chance!" The line went dead.

Clay felt pretty much the same way.

"EVERYBODY COME QUICK!"

The teenage girl's voice broke Niki's concentration and she looked up from the pan of fresh green beans in her lap. Granny, stirring potato salad in an enormous stainless steel bowl, frowned.

"Is anything wrong, Missy?"

The redhead from Kansas City shook her head fiercely. "No, but you won't want to miss this!"

Niki's heart sank. She put the pan on the counter. "What is it?"

"Clay's going to show us some Roman riding! I'm not sure what that is, but Dobe says nobody'll want to miss it so *come on!*"

The slamming of the kitchen door announced her departure.

"Oh, dear." Grandma sounded worried. "You don't suppose that boy's really going to ride standing up, do you?"

"I wouldn't be at all surprised." Niki wondered how he kept finding new ways to make her crazy.

Or perhaps the word was *crazier*, because she was already fairly crazed from the unrelenting pressure of Clay and his cohorts, all bent on convincing her to change her mind before it was too late. Last night she'd lain in bed for hours, trying to convince herself that the best thing to do was to simply get in her car and drive to...to San Antonio, Corpus Christi, anywhere she could hide out until the Queen of the Cowgirls was chosen.

Now this. Clay was going to ride two horses simultaneously, standing with one foot on the back of each? She could at least see that he had a decent funeral.

Grimly, she untied her apron and tossed it onto the countertop. Outside, she found everyone—dudes and cowboys alike—clustered around the fence circling the training arena. With dragging steps, she joined the throng, wondering why she was putting herself through this.

What if he was hurt...again? She'd seen his naked body and knew he was no stranger to pain, but that didn't ease her fears. Horses! Why did people have to mess with them? They were so big and smelly and stupid and—

"There he goes!" The lady from Alabama pointed. "He's standing up!"

Niki had to see. Moving to a vacant section of the wooden pole fence, she climbed up until she could look over the top.

Sure enough, Clay stood on the backs of two ranch horses, a black and a bay. The animals moved along at a smart trot, side by side, although not in step. The man was getting a rough ride of it, but seemed in perfect control, smiling at his appreciative audience and showboating for all he was worth.

"Faster!" the redheaded teen called, cupping her hands around her mouth. "Go faster!"

Oh, shut up! Niki thought, but she didn't say it. She didn't figure Clay really needed much encouragement.

The horses broke into a gallop. For a moment, Clay's right boot seemed to slip, but he caught himself and the trio thundered past to great applause.

Dylan crawled up on the fence beside Niki.

"Damn, he's good," the young cowboy said admiringly. "I tried that a couple of times and fell on my ass—'er the ground."

"He may fall on his...ground if he doesn't slow down," Niki said tightly. Climbing to the top rail, she swung her leg over to sit astride. "Darn, that black horse is drifting. Clay's going to be doing the splits if he's not careful."

And he might have, except at the last minute he dropped to a sitting position on the black horse, gathered in his reins and then released the reins of the bay. As if on cue, the black whirled in a circle and reared up on hind legs.

It was a beautiful sight, the man as secure and easy on the horse as if they were one. While the black's legs pawed the air, Clay lifted his hat and waved it to the crowd.

A deep, appreciative *ahhhh!* swept the audience, followed by enthusiastic applause. The horse dropped back down on all fours and Clay clapped his heels against the animal's sides. With a mighty thrust of powerful hindquarters, the horse jumped forward, heading straight for the fence.

Niki gasped and leaned away, clinging to the rough board for balance. Was the horse out of control? It looked as if he might smash into the rail fence and kill both of them.

Instead, Clay pulled the horse up just short of disaster. The animal danced in a circle, neck arched and eyes flashing. Niki, on a level with those eyes, could hardly breathe. Frozen to the spot, she stared at her worst nightmare: a horse, close enough to finish the job started by his kin all those years ago.

She didn't know what Clay intended until his arm clamped around her waist in an iron grip. Terrified, she jerked her attention away from the horse.

"Turn loose!" Clay ordered.

"Turn—?"

"Of the fence. Turn loose of the fence."

Automatically she did as he directed, once she understood him. "But why? *Aargh!*"

For he swept her off her perch and pulled her tight against his chest. Holding her there, he whirled the horse and kicked him into a dead run.

All Niki could do was cling to Clay and pray she'd live long enough to kill him.

HE LEANED DOWN and whispered in her ear. "This is called riding off into the sunset."

She uttered a strangled sound without raising her face, buried against his chest. Her hands gripped his shirt so tightly he thought she might rip it.

It'd be worth losing a good shirt if this worked out the way he hoped. Surely after seeing him showboating on horseback, after being carried off as romantically as he could manage, after realizing how nice horses could be, she'd start seeing them in a whole new light.

He was desperate enough to hope so.

The black moved over familiar trails at a steady lope. Clay found it relatively easy to keep his balance bareback even with Niki draped across the animal's withers like a sack of grain. With every step, his spirits rose.

At least she wasn't screaming hysterically. Maybe this really would work. If it did, he'd be a happy camper because this was his idea of courting: a horse under him, the wind in his face, and a woman he...cared about a great deal in his arms.

The black was slowing, finally easing into a quick trot, a much rougher gait. Niki stirred in his arms and he leaned down to murmur soothing words in her ears.

"Everything's fine, just relax. There's nothing to worry about...I've got you. See how easy this is? There's nothing to be afraid of."

She didn't respond except to twist her fingers more securely in his shirtfront. Silken black hair whipped across his face and he savored the sting of it because it was *hers*. Beautiful, sexy Niki...

She burrowed her face deeper into his chest. "Can we just *stop* now?"

"Sure, if you want to." He pulled the black up, thinking that she'd seemed unexpectedly calm when she asked it. "You okay?"

She didn't answer so he just sat there holding her, thinking that life didn't get much better than this.

Letting his head drop back, he looked up through the leafy leaves of a cottonwood tree. A faint breeze brushed his cheek and sunlight lay dappled around him.

Maybe he should ask her to marry him.

That unexpected thought pierced him like an arrow. He'd never proposed marriage to a woman, any woman. He'd proposed lots of other things but never the big *M*, the long haul, forever and ever. Of course, he'd never known a woman like Niki before. Look how she'd adjusted to his little prank.

This was turning out just fine. Someday she'd thank him for freeing her of her phobia. Someday after they'd been married for ten, twenty years...

She lifted her head and looked at him with haunted eyes. Snatched from his blissful reverie, Clay stiffened.

"What is it, honey? I thought—"

"The hell you did!" She shoved her hands against him and pushed. "Clay Russell, I will never, ever forgive you for this as long as I live!"

And then she tumbled off the horse backwards.

10

Niki lay on the soft earth, stunned to find herself looking up at the silhouette of man and beast towering above her. Sunlight through the trees nearly blinded her and she closed her eyes, struggling to catch her breath.

The sound of Clay's boots hitting the earth was followed by the pawing of the horse's hooves. Cowering, she tried to open her eyes again, but couldn't quite manage it.

She sensed movement, then Clay was beside her, touching her, demanding to know if she was all right, if she'd hurt herself.

She finally got her breath back and her eyes snapped open. "Like you care, you monster!" Rolling out of his arms, she came up groggily onto her knees.

"Why'd you jump out of my arms that way?" His voice was strangled, anxious. "You could have been hurt."

"You think I wasn't?" She lifted her head, trying to glare at him past the curtain of hair. "I could have been killed! I could have died of shock! How dare you do that to me?"

"Because—" He rocked back on his heels. "I thought it was romantic," he admitted sheepishly.

"Romantic! Are you mad?" Somehow she managed to stagger to her feet. She didn't think anything was broken, but took her time shaking out each extremity. "Especially since you know perfectly well how I feel about horses."

He looked both confused and uncomfortable. "Yeah, but I didn't think you meant it," he said lamely. "I mean, I know you *thought* you meant it when you said you hate horses, but that just isn't...it isn't *natural*. I...uh...thought I was doing you a favor, to tell you the truth."

"A *favor!*" Fury bubbled in her chest, giving her the strength to take a tottering step. "Are you out of your mind? I'm *happy* hating horses. What do I care if you don't like it?"

He frowned. "But I thought—" He clamped his teeth together.

"Did you really?" She draped her arm around a small tree and sagged against it. Her strength was slowly returning, but she still felt shaky and disoriented. "I can't wait to hear this."

He licked his lips. "Ah, hell, I just thought that was the real reason you didn't want to go to Dallas for the Cowgirl contest, the fact that you were afraid to ride a horse."

"Clay Russell," she said indignantly, "you're out of your mind. I didn't want to go because *I hate beauty contests!* They're demeaning and offensive and I don't want any part of them. I never did. I think that anyone who'd buy a product because some dim-bulb model told them too is *demented.*"

"But Niki—"

"Yes, I know, you've been hawking Mother Hubbard's line, and I'm sorry if I've offended you—" She caught her breath and glared at him anew. "No, I'm not sorry! Why should I be? I never asked you to come here and turn my life upside down. I never asked you to force your way into my home—"

"And your bed. Don't forget your bed."

"Ohhh!" She closed her eyes for a moment to collect herself. "Why don't you go ride a bull? Or sell a carload of jeans? Or—"

"Niki, will you just shut up and listen for a minute?" He fixed her with a pleading gaze. "There's something I want to ask you, although why I should after all this I don't know."

"The answer is, forget it."

"You don't even know the question."

"The hell I don't! The next person who so much as mentions that damned contest is going to get a fat lip."

"But—"

"Leave me alone, Clay!"

Shoving herself away from the tree, she hobbled

back down the trail, giving the grazing black horse a wide berth.

"Hang on a minute," he called after her. "I brought you here and I'll take you back."

"On that beast? I don't think so." She kept walking...limping.

She could hear his movements as he caught up the horse and sprang onto its back. Thank heaven! All she wanted was for him to go away and leave her alone.

He didn't. Something soft touched her shoulder blade and she jumped a foot in the air, then whirled to confront him. The horse's head was down, so close that she was literally eyeball to eyeball with him. She started back, her hands balling into fists.

"Did that animal just try to bite me?"

"Of course not. He gave you a friendly little nudge to get your attention."

The horse did have a curious expression on its vicious bony face. "Keep it away from me," she cried, retreating further. "I warn you, if you pull any more funny stuff, I'll...I'll call the police."

"You won't call the police because you'd be a laughingstock," he said reasonably. "This is *Texas*. Horses and hound dogs are a way of life."

"Not to me, they're not. You noticed that scar on the back of my knee."

"So?"

"My leg was broken—shattered, actually, by a

horse. Or maybe I should say several horses. I was only five at the time so I wasn't counting."

"Ah, Jeez, Niki, I'm sorry."

Numbly she pressed on. "Remember me telling you how much like my mother I am? A horse killed her—threw her and dragged her. I was only seven, but I was there. I saw it. My sisters didn't, but I did."

"Ah, Niki—"

His anguished tone didn't compute with her, not now. She was too upset. "Go away, Clay," she cried in a voice that trembled. "We're finished for good. You might as well give up and go home because *nothing* could get me on a horse voluntarily."

When she turned and walked away, he didn't follow. By the time she reached the ranch house, her eyes were nearly dry again.

CLAY FELT lower than a snake's belly. His plan had not only backfired, it had backfired big time. She probably *wouldn't* speak to him again. Under the circumstances, he couldn't very well blame her.

He skipped dinner that night, too depressed to put on a happy face. But later he made a point of tracking Grandma down while she was loading the dishwasher.

"Can I talk to you for a few minutes, Mrs. Collins?" He couldn't quite manage a smile.

"Sure can." She cocked her sweet face to look at

him. "You missed dinner. Would you like me to fix you a plate?"

"No, thanks." He hadn't even thought about food. "It's about..." He couldn't bring himself to say her name.

He didn't have to. "Niki," Granny supplied, nodding wisely. "My goodness, you did make a tactical error with that stunt this afternoon."

He hung his head, ashamed. "I guess I did, but I thought..." He sighed. "I don't suppose it matters what I thought."

"Now, now, it just might." She looked sympathetic, at least. "You've got to understand that she has good reason for how she feels."

"She told me."

Granny's blue eyes widened. "About her mother?"

He nodded. "She says she's a lot like her mother."

"In looks, maybe."

"Other ways, too." He caught himself; Niki had said she'd never told her family about her early misadventures and he wouldn't betray her now. "Whatever. She also confirmed what you told me about getting hurt by horses when she was a little bitty thing."

Granny nodded. "She got stomped pretty good. For a while we thought she'd always walk with a limp but she seems to have come back okay."

He remembered Niki limping down the trail ahead of him and felt sick with remorse. "I didn't know her fear was still so strong when I kidnapped her. I figured it would be...hell, I thought she'd think it was romantic."

"And you're feeling pretty doggoned romantic toward her these days or I miss my guess."

Shrewd old lady. He nodded. "She's...really something."

"She is that."

"But I haven't been able to talk her into going on with the contest."

"You just haven't found the right way to approach her yet."

The flicker of hope was completely unexpected. "Can you give me a clue what the right way might be?"

"Mercy, no!" Granny smiled ruefully. "I don't give advice to the lovelorn."

He managed a half-hearted grin. "Do I look lovelorn?"

"You do to me." She closed the dishwasher and gave him a comforting pat on the shoulder. "Cheer up, Clay. Sometimes you have to back off and give a person room to think."

Later that night, when he saw Niki across the campfire, he remembered Granny's words. Maybe it *was* time for him to pull out, to give Niki room to think.

But first...

Working his way through the crowd, he sidled up

to her and sat down on the log next to her. He could sense the way she pulled back, as much mentally and physically, when she saw him.

He leaned forward and picked up a stick with which to poke at the fire. After a while he said, "I'm really sorry."

"Are you." Her voice was completely without inflection.

"God knows I am." It was almost a groan. "It was a dumb thing to do and I'm sorry I scared you. Please accept my apology."

"All right." In moonlight and firelight, her face remained expressionless.

"I'll be leaving tomorrow."

She stiffened almost imperceptibly, but he saw it and his heart raced. Now was the time for her to turn to him and say she understood, that she truly forgave him and perhaps they could try—

"I think that might be best," she said, still cool and calm. Rising, she looked down. "Have a good trip and drive carefully."

She walked away, taking his last chance with her. For a moment he thought of calling her back, of explaining how important this was not only to her future but to his as well, telling her he loved her and wanted to marry her—

Hell, there it was again!

She'd laugh in his face, of course. She'd think he'd

stooped to a new low to get his way. She'd hate him even more than she did already.

He was tough, but not that tough. He might as well pack and get it over with.

CLAY WAS really going to do it.

He couldn't get his own way, so he was actually going to wash his hands of the whole thing. Despite the fact that she'd encouraged just such a conclusion, Niki was crushed to realize it was actually going to happen.

He said his goodbyes to the current crop of dudes at breakfast. A spontaneous murmur of disappointment swept the dining room and it seemed that everyone made a point of shaking his hand on the way out.

Niki, of course, was the exception. As soon as she could slip away, she planted herself behind the desk in the Great Room to tackle the bills. She'd no more than got started when Dani strolled in, Elsie in her arms and father-in-law Travis in tow.

Travis waved and headed on through to the kitchen, but Dani planted herself in front of the desk. "How's it goin', sis?"

Niki shrugged. "Okay. How's my favorite niece?"

"Your *only* niece is doing just fine these days. That stubborn tooth finally came in, thank heaven." She planted a kiss on the curly head. Elsie giggled and struggled to get free. "Excuse us. I promised Granny I'd help her bake pies today so I'd better get to it."

Dani carried her wiggly child away. Niki watched wistfully. She envied her sister—actually, she envied *both* her sisters. With her luck, she thought glumly, she'd likely end up an old maid. Miss Maiden Aunt of America—now there was a title she *really* didn't want.

Clay came down the stairs, suitcase in hand. Niki straightened and gave him a cool smile.

"Leaving already?"

"No more reason to stay." He crossed to her and dropped a check on the desk. "This should clear my bill."

She frowned. "You've worked for your keep. Isn't this a bit of overkill?"

"No." He seemed glum when he said it. "I know I put everyone out by movin' in here. In retrospect, I regret doing it. Guess you could say the check's to cover the aggravation factor."

Offended, she stared down at the piece of paper. Although generous, it would have to be for a million dollars to cover her aggravation. Finally she just said, "All right," and slid the check into the drawer. Keeping her expression bland, she added, "Was there anything else?"

Their gazes caught and held and she felt that old familiar dart of lightning down her spine. Her mouth opened on an involuntary gasp, but she stubbornly pressed her lips together.

After a moment, he straightened. "No, I guess there isn't anything else...well, maybe one final thing. The actual contest is day after tomorrow at two o'clock at Eve's ranch outside Dallas. I took the liberty of drawing you a map." Reaching into his pocket, he hauled out a folded piece of paper and dropped it on the desk.

She didn't pick it up, just sat there looking at it and feeling as if he'd landed one final blow.

He leaned forward, his expression intense and his palms braced on the desktop. "Remember the first time we spoke at the Sorry Bastard? I told you there was nothing there I wanted."

"I remember."

"I was wrong. There was something I wanted and I came back to get it."

Confused, she lifted her chin. "What are you saying, Clay?"

"There doesn't seem to be anything at Eve's ranch that *you* want but you might change your mind. If you do, come."

"I'll be sure to do that." Said with cool derision. Hadn't they beat this into the ground already?

"That's that, then. Goodbye, Niki. Thanks for everything." For another long, tense moment, he regarded her with...perhaps it was regret. Then he turned and walked out of the house.

And suddenly the realization that she might never see him again crashed down on her like an avalanche.

SHE WASN'T GOING TO STOP HIM.

He'd thought she would. He'd believed that when she realized he was really going, she'd do something—*anything.*

He'd been wrong. Now he had to go on back to Dallas and face the music—Eve—and do some serious thinking about his future. He, who always took things as they came, now found himself between a rock and a hard place.

No rodeo, no big advertising contract, no girl.

Yippee! Looked like it was just about time to start all over again.

"GOOD GRIEF! What's this?"

A gentle hand touched the back of Niki's head, resting on her arms on the desk. Grandma. Please don't let Dani be with her!

"What's the matter, Niki?" Dani; so much for prayer. "I saw you not ten minutes ago and you were fine. What the heck's happened? Why are you crying?"

Niki drew a deep breath, rubbed her wet eyes with her forearms and lifted her head. She sniffled and swallowed hard. "I'm not crying," she croaked.

"Of course you're crying," Dani said. She looked

worried. "That's not against the law, for goodness' sake. Just tell us what's wrong so we can help you."

Granny brushed a callused thumb across Niki's damp cheekbones. "Calm down, Dani. Let her catch her breath." Turning, she drew up a chair. "Did you just say goodbye to Clay, dear?"

Niki nodded, keeping her face averted, hoping they wouldn't notice how her lips trembled.

"Did that no-good bum—"

"Dani!" Niki glared at her sister. "He's not a no-good bum."

"Oh, no?" Dani did not look convinced. "Then why are you crying?"

"Because—oh, I don't know why! I never wanted Clay here, I never wanted anything to do with that stupid contest, I never wanted anything in my life to change. Now it feels as if everything's just...just upside down."

Granny patted Niki's hand, but she spoke to Dani. "She's never been in love before," she said, "not really. That's why she's so confused."

Dani's jaw dropped. "In love! Are you kidding?"

Both of them turned to Niki for confirmation or denial.

Niki swallowed hard. "I'm not in love...am I?"

Dani laughed incredulously. "You aren't sure?"

"I am," Granny said. "I'm sorry you didn't stop him from going, Niki, but it's not too late."

"I couldn't stop him from going!" Niki stared at

her grandmother. "He's a grown man. He does what he wants."

"Like you do? You *wanted* to stop him, now admit it."

"Well, maybe...yes, all right, I wanted him to stay. But it had to be his decision."

"It's hard to make an intelligent decision when you don't have all the facts," Granny said gently. "And he didn't, because you didn't tell him you love him."

"How could I, even if I do, which is still in doubt, until I have some idea how he feels about me?"

Dani sat down hard on a straight-backed chair. "I'm getting confused. I had no idea things had gone so far between you and Clay."

Niki slumped over the desk. "I didn't mean it to go anywhere," she said plaintively. "He just kept coming back and after a while..." She chewed on her lip. "Then he just gave up and now he's gone and that's that, and I feel *awful*."

"You should tell him how you feel," Granny said.

"But I don't know how I feel, except awful, that is." Niki clenched her hands into impotent fists. "I'd probably just make a fool of myself."

"When you love someone," Dani said suddenly, "you don't worry about making a fool of yourself, you just worry about the other person's happiness."

"Really?" Niki looked at her sister with wide eyes.

"Is that the test of love, when someone else is more important to you than you are?"

"That's *my* test," Dani said, serious now instead of flailing away with words. "It's the same way I feel about my child. It's wanting to give more than you take. It's—"

The telephone rang. Rolling her eyes, Dani answered, listened, frowned, said, "Just a minute, I'll see if she's available."

Niki's stomach clenched; could it be Clay? She practically ripped the phone from her sister's hand.

Eve's voice punctured Niki's balloon. "Hello, dear. I just spoke to Clay and he tells me I have to get your final decision from you, not him. This leads me to believe you still haven't definitely decided about the contest."

Niki caught her breath; he hadn't told his boss that the final decision was a resounding *no*.

Which meant it could still be *yes*.

"I..." She stumbled for careful words. "I'm still considering."

"Really." Eve did not sound pleased. "I'm assuming Clay explained to you what his own status will be if you don't make the right decision."

"His status?"

"As spokesman for Mother Hubbard."

Niki frowned. "I guess he didn't mention that."

"I'm surprised because this could be just the straw to push you in the right direction. You see, if you

don't show up here, Clay's going to be out of a job."
Her laughter was not convincing. "I promised
twelve contestants and by God, there had better be
twelve contestants here day after tomorrow."

"If only eleven show up, that won't be Clay's
fault."

"I'm not talking fault, I'm talking economics. I'm
talking an advertising campaign that's on its last
legs. I'm talking...*you*."

A cold shiver ran down Niki's spine. "Even if I
show up, I may not win," she said desperately.
"There are judges, after all, and unless you're planning to fix the contest—"

"Heaven forbid," Eve interrupted lightly. "Have
to run now, but think about what I've said."

Niki hung up the handset slowly, her mind awhirl.
Clay's job depended upon her showing up? But he
hadn't said—

Of course, he hadn't. He wouldn't try to manipulate her that way. Persuasion was one thing, but emo-
tional blackmail was quite another.

"Mercy," Granny exclaimed, "you're white as a
sheet. What happened?"

"I'm...not sure." She bit her lip anxiously. "I think
I've just been had."

"How so?" Dani wanted to know.

"That was Eve Hubbard. She says if I don't show
up for that blasted contest, she's going to axe the en-

tire campaign and that would mean Clay's out of a job."

Dani shrugged. "He'll be going back to rodeo soon so it won't be such a big deal."

"That's just it. He may not be going back to rodeo, for medical reasons. This could be a big blow to him."

The three women sat in silence. Then Dani said, "You've changed your mind, then. You're going to do it."

"How can I?" Niki's voice cracked with strain. "I suppose I could stand being judged like a cow, but I can't get up on a horse in front of a bunch of strangers." She shuddered at the image. "I can't ride a horse, period. But if it will save the future of the man...the man I l-love—oh, what am I going to do?"

"Take Sundance," Dani offered.

Sundance was Dani's treasured Appaloosa, her pet, her personal horse, ridden by no one else. "I couldn't do that," Niki said, aware of her sister's territorial attitudes.

"You've got to," Dani disagreed. "Anybody can ride that Appaloosa, assuming I let them, even you. I could make you at least *look* like a cowgirl in about fifteen minutes, assuming you won't panic and start screaming. Sundance hates screaming."

Niki remained unconvinced. "What if, God forbid, I should win? What would I do if I had to keep up the pretense that I'm a cowgirl for an entire year?"

"We'll cross that bridge when we come to it," Dani said. "Besides, you might lose—" Niki's eyes flew wide. "Nah, not a chance. You always win."

"This time, winning would mean losing." Niki shook her head helplessly. "Besides that, how would I get Sundance to Dallas? I can't drag a horse trailer all that way by myself."

She'd found an out. It couldn't be done. She'd tried to think of a way to save Clay's job and failed. She'd done her best.

Just then Travis Burke walked through the front door with his granddaughter in his arms. He took one look at the tableau before him and asked, "What are you women up to this time?"

Dani glanced at him, then smiled at her daughter. "We've got a little problem. Niki needs to be in Dallas day after tomorrow for the Queen of the Cowgirls contest and we're trying to figure out how to get Sundance there, too."

Travis's eyes narrowed thoughtfully. "That's Eve's big deal, right?"

Dani nodded.

"And the contest will be held at her ranch, right?"

Dani nodded again.

"Hmm..."

Now all three looked at Travis with varying degrees of curiosity. Dani said, "I suppose we could ask Dylan or someone like that to drive her...."

"No need," Travis said crisply. Leaning over, he

set Elsie on the floor. She promptly took off at top speed for the kitchen. Granny scooped her up before she could make the dining room door.

Travis didn't seem to notice. "I've got unfinished business with Eve Hubbard," he said in a voice that boded ill for that lady. "How about I drive you, Niki?"

Everybody looked at Niki, who shrank back in her chair. There she was, hoist with her own petard.

She hesitated, her future hanging in the balance....

11

"WHAT THE HELL!" Niki jumped up, swept by a wave of determination that made it impossible to sit still a moment longer. "What have I got to lose except my self-respect and maybe my life?"

"Huh?" Travis frowned. "I thought this was a beauty contest."

"It is." Laughing, Dani came around to hug her sister. "We can do this. Trust me."

Niki liked the "we." The Keene triplets always came through for each other in a pinch. "Grandma?" She turned to the old lady sitting quietly beside the desk with the toddler on her lap. "Am I crazy?"

"Honey, you're in love." Grandma's broad grin lit up the room. "That just *seems* like the same thing."

Travis scuffed his boots against the floor impatiently. "So we goin' to Dallas or not?"

"We're going."

"When?"

Niki looked at Dani for guidance. "When? I've g-got to get acquainted with Sundance..." She swallowed hard, the meaning of what she'd just agreed to do sinking in. But she wouldn't waver—she wouldn't!

"We'll do that tomorrow," Dani, always willing to take charge, decided. "You can also pack tomorrow and leave early the next morning."

"Is that enough time?" It was hard to get the words out past the panic fluttering in Niki's belly.

"Just barely, but that's got to be better than getting there too early. You won't have time to think—always a good thing in a pinch. Get in, compete, get out. Wham, bam, thank you, ma'am."

Niki managed a shaky smile. "I'm sure you're right. Is that okay with you, Travis?"

"Fine and dandy, but we'll have to get out of here early. Tell you what. I'll go on over to the XOX, load up that Appaloosa and bring him on over here now."

"That's great, Travis." Dani patted her father-in-law on the arm. "Thanks."

"Yes, thanks," Niki echoed, wondering what she'd done to herself this time.

NIKI TOOK a faltering step forward. Sundance gave her a curious glance but didn't move another muscle.

Dani spoke encouragingly. "That's right, Nik. See how calm he is? Now pat his neck."

"Pat his neck?" Niki licked her lips, but kept her arms stiff at her sides.

Dani demonstrated, stroking the sleek animal. "You want to make friends," she explained. "Think of him as...as a big dog! You like dogs and they're more dangerous than horses."

"I doubt that. No dog ever ran over me." Niki laid a shaky hand alongside Sundance's neck. "Now what?"

"Now you put your left foot in the stirrup and climb into the saddle."

The moment of truth had arrived. Niki stared at the Appaloosa, her nerve threatening to fail. It was time to do or die. How much did she want to do this thing for Clay?

Enough to take this chance and a million more. Gritting her teeth, she reached for the saddle horn.

"AND I WAS real impressed the way you crawled up on that horse," Travis said, glancing over his shoulder at Niki for emphasis. "You got guts, girl."

"Thanks." She said it wryly, thinking that what she'd done took a lot more than guts; it took love. And it would take a lot more of the same to get her back in the saddle, but she was committed now, at least in her mind.

They'd been on the road to Dallas for about five hours. One more hour was all that that lay between Niki and her future, whatever it might turn out to be. She was going to have to try to stay on board a horse, which she'd sworn never to do, and smile and answer inane questions in pursuit of a title she desperately didn't want to win.

Hardest of all, she must steel herself to confess her love for a man about whose feelings she was uncertain. None of this would be easy, but at least she wouldn't be scuttling his career.

His happiness was more important to her than her own. It *had* to be love.

"You got that map?"

Travis's voice startled her out of her unhappy reverie. "Yes."

"We're gettin' close to our turn. Can you check which highway we're lookin' for?"

She did, referring to the hand-drawn map provided by Clay. They drove on for a few minutes of silence and then she said, "This is awfully nice of you, Travis."

He let out an unintelligible grunt. "Not so nice."

"It certainly is," she insisted firmly.

"What it is is selfish. I needed an excuse to see her again and you just gave it to me."

Niki knew who "she" was. "You and Eve seemed to hit it off pretty well," she ventured.

He shrugged. "Yeah, at first. But then she got on her high horse and said I was taking her for granted—for granted, hell! How do you take someone for granted when you've only known 'em for twenty-four hours?"

She laughed. "That's a toughie."

"She said if I didn't come around before she left the Bar-K, that was it, that was all she wrote. And I told *her* if she didn't at least call me before she headed back to Dallas, I'd figure she was just another big city kook out to take advantage of us local yokels."

"Do I sense an impasse?"

"Yeah, up to now. But I've been missin' her so much..." He sighed. "I was just lookin' for an excuse and you gave me one, for which I thank you. I don't know whether this will lead to anything in particular, but I do know I gotta take a chance and find out. She's something special. Whatever it is we've got goin', I don't want to just let it slip away without trying to figure it out."

Niki nodded, thinking that she didn't, either. She had to take a chance to figure out whatever it was she had going with Clay.

For the first time in a very long time, Travis's words gave her a kind of peace with what she intended to do.

Soon he was maneuvering the truck and trailer into the right lane and onto a highway heading east. Once back in the flow of traffic, he glanced at his silent passenger. "You're getting nervous."

"Yes." She bit her lip.

"When we get there, you just take off and find out where you're supposed to be and what you're supposed to be doing. I'll unload Sundance and get him all ready for you."

"Th-thanks, Travis."

"Niki, don't worry. Dani's right, anybody can ride that horse a'hers. If he has to, ol' Sundance will reach around and *hold* you in the saddle."

Imagining that, she laughed. "It may come to that."

"Hon," he said, "you've been around riders all your life. Just pretend you're Dani or Toni and everything will be fine. Trust ol' Sundance. Hell, he's smarter than most people I know."

Niki couldn't argue with *that*.

CLAY JUST KEPT SMILING.

He'd been smiling for the last two days, ever since the contestants for Queen of the Cowgirls started arriving at Eve's palatial ranch house on the WWD spread. That's when the flashbulbs started popping. He didn't mind having his picture taken, but he couldn't stop the word "overkill" leaping into his mind.

Eve's place was a marvel and well worth any attention that came its way. It had everything, including an indoor arena where the Mother Hubbard's Wild West Duds fashion shoots were always held.

Barns and corrals, all perfectly matched and maintained, surrounded the central compound with its massive southern mansion-style house. Eve kept several horses, but they were for guests, publicity and photo props. She didn't ride herself although she expected everyone else to.

"Clay! Yoo-hoo!" Grace Stanley, the contestant from Tulsa, waved and blew kisses while camera strobes flashed. Clay smiled back, but it was automatic.

After spending the past two days here, he was growing tired and distracted. The actual contest would begin in about fifteen minutes when the contestants would ride into the arena on a hay wagon wearing clothing from Mother Hubbard's latest collection. They'd be judged in each category by a three-member panel fully prepared to vote any which way Eve told them to. Then the contestants would move on to personal interviews, a grand parade on horseback, and final appearances in Mother's new line of western evening wear.

All eleven of them lusted after that title with all the perks and publicity that came with it. More than a few also seemed to lust after *him*, but Clay wasn't interested. He'd do his job, go through the motions, but he was off women as a whole and one in particular. If he never got involved with another one of 'em, it would be too soon.

Photographers moved into new positions. The audience in the bleachers, mostly made up of locals and the friends and family of contestants, stirred expectantly. Lights went down and photographers moved into place around the entrance to the arena. Eve's magnified voice suddenly reverberated through the arena.

"Welcome to our Queen of the Cowgirls competition, ladies and gentlemen. We're about to select a beautiful new face to represent Mother Hubbard's Wild West Duds, the foremost brand of western wear in the world. Our winner will have to be more than beautiful, actually, because as our spokeswoman she'll be representing us all across the country while serving as a role model for today's youth. Obviously, she must be a very special young woman.

"Now sit back and prepare to be impressed. Ladies and gentlemen, presenting our twelve contestants for the title of Queen of the Cowgirls."

Clay noted her number faux pas and groaned. He knew perfectly well there were only eleven contestants and so did she. She must be more stressed out than he'd realized.

Large floor-to-roof doors swung open at one end of the arena and a large hay wagon appeared, pulled by giant Clydesdale horses. Lifting their big shaggy feet, they hauled the wagon effortlessly around the arena while contestants perched on hay bales waved enthusiastically to the cheering crowd.

At least, eleven of the contestants were enthusiastic. One of them seemed only belatedly to realize what was required of her, despite the fact that Eve had personally briefed everyone just a few hours ago.

He frowned. There was something so familiar

about the set of the shoulders, the tilt of the head and the—

Jeez, she lifted her hat to the crowd and a silken waterfall of black hair cascaded over her shoulders. Niki. That was Niki! By some miracle, Niki was here and she was competing. What in the name of God could have changed her mind?

And then he knew. Eve must have told her that Clay was about to get the boot and she'd come out of guilt.

Great. He stood there feeling like somebody's poor relation, waiting for the wagon to roll to a stop so he could offer his hand to each contestant as she alighted. All he could think about was Niki and what this was costing her.

But he'd won.

He felt like hell.

NIKI PUT OUT HER HAND and Clay took it in a grip so powerful that she gasped.

"Sorry," he muttered under his breath, escorting her to the bottom of the ramp that had been rolled into place at the end of the wagon.

No smile, no wink, no welcome at all. She felt the knot that was her stomach compress even more. Feeling stupid in denim shorts and boots, she took her place with the other contestants, trying to smile and act as if she were happy just to be here.

And this was just the beginning. She still had that horse thing to get past.

When her name was called, she did what the others had done: step forward, smile, pivot slowly, walk right, walk left, return to the line. Then it was back onto the hay wagon while a western band played lively music and the contestants smiled and blew kisses.

Niki thought she might be sick.

CLAY WAITED, grim-faced, to lift Niki from the hay wagon. This he did to the accompaniment of glares from most of the other contestants. Anxious and unhappy, Niki let him drag her into a narrow passageway where he confronted her.

"What the hell are you doing here?" His voice was strident.

"I—" Words weren't going to do the trick. She just threw herself against his chest, her arms rising to wrap around his neck. "I came because I love you, Clay," she cried.

His arms jerked as if with a spasm, then closed around her so tightly she gasped. "Am I hearing things?" The strident tone was gone, replaced by one of disbelief. "You love me? You really do?"

He hadn't repeated her pledge of love, but she dared not weaken in her resolve to be honest with him. She nodded, her head bumping up beneath his chin. "I love you and I'm willing to do whatever I can to save your future with Mother Hubbard."

He went still and the pressure of his arms loosened around her. "Eve told you about that?"

"Yes." She leaned back so she could see his face.

"Look, if I lose this job I won't exactly be destitute. I've got a lot of options, so I'm letting you off the hook." Dropping his arms, he stepped away, his face as blank and hard as marble.

Panic gripped her. "What if I don't want off the hook?"

"Come on, Niki!" He shook his head. "You're looking forward to climbing on a horse and riding out into that arena? I don't think so."

Her mouth had gone dry and her hands felt cold and clammy. "Of course I'm not looking forward to it," she said defensively, "but I'm w-willing to do my best. I've got to, or forever consider myself a coward." She gave an anxious little laugh. "I'll probably lose anyway so I'll only have to do it once."

"Dream on."

"What?"

"The fix is in, Niki. All you have to do to win this is not fall off your horse."

"What!" Her heart leaped into her throat and she gasped. "You mean—"

"*Niki!*" Travis bulled around the corner. "Jeez, here you are. C'mon, they're waiting for you. You, too, Clay. Eve's on the warpath."

"Travis?" Clay's eyes narrowed. "What the hell do you have to do with this?"

"Nothin' much," the rancher said. "Just bein' neighborly. Here." He thrust a pair of bright purple jeans at her. "Put these on and let's go. Sundance is ready, willin' and able."

For a moment she stood there, holding the jeans and fighting panic. She couldn't do this! She especially couldn't do it if she was going to win, for God's sake. Maybe Clay was wrong. She looked at him, needing support.

"You don't *have* to do this," he said.

And that's when she knew for sure that she did.

"OKAY, SUNDANCE." Niki touched the Appaloosa's bony forehead with a hesitant hand. "It's just you and me, fella. You won't let me down, will you?"

The horse's great dark eyes flickered.

"I'll take that as a no."

"Will you just *get on?*" The man in charge of the proceedings appeared at her elbow, clipboard in hand.

Easy for him to say. He had on a suit, and from the way he steered clear of Sundance, he probably knew less about horses than she did.

Travis stepped forward. "Let me boost you up. Keep your feet in the stirrups and a loose rein. Sundance will know what to do. And if you let him—"

He smiled up at her, secure in the saddle before

she even knew what was happening. He thrust her left boot into the stirrup.

"—and if you let him, he'll make you look good."

"I'll let him, I'll let him!" She grasped the big saddle horn with one hand and took a deep breath. "I'm ready."

"Then let 'er rip!"

Travis slapped Sundance on the rump and stepped aside.

She was on her own.

CLAY SAT next to Eve in the VIP box, holding his breath. He couldn't believe Niki was even attempting this, after the way she'd reacted when he'd tried to carry her off on horseback.

Sundance galloped majestically into the arena with Niki clinging to the saddle like a cocklebur. The crowd roared and she jerked as if she'd been struck physically. The Appaloosa didn't so much as alter his steady stride.

She was doing great, Clay realized, his utter fear slowly giving way to pride and admiration. Apparently sensing that the worst was past, she straightened in the saddle, her long black hair streaming out behind her like a silken banner.

Woman and horse loped around the arena to take their place in the line of cowgirls waiting in the middle—the best of the best. Apparently the audience agreed because the smattering of applause grew until it rolled and echoed through the arena.

Damn, she didn't need a fixed contest to win. She was so vastly superior to the other contestants that any fool could see it.

Travis appeared and Eve welcomed the tall rancher with a broad smile. "We meet again," she said in a low, sexy voice.

"Hell, Eve, you used that line on me not fifteen minutes ago."

"That's right, I did. You've done a wonderful job with Niki, by the way."

"I didn't do a damn thing except haul that horse up here." He looked her up and down. "You and me have got some talking to do."

"Later, darling. I want to see—"

"Now."

"Travis, don't be contumacious."

"I'm not." He frowned. "What the hell is contumacious?"

"Why—" She looked taken aback. "It means insubordinate."

"I'm that all right." He grabbed her hand. "Let's go."

"But—"

"Eve, it's now or never."

They stood there staring into each other's eyes. Clay, who was pretty sure how this was going to end, turned back to the woman sitting with perfect confidence on the speckled horse in the middle of the arena. When Travis and Eve walked away, he didn't even look around.

"I DID IT! I DID IT!"

Niki threw her right leg over the cantle and slid out of the saddle into Clay's waiting arms. "No matter what happens now, I've conquered *that* fear. I doubt I'll ever be the horse lover my sisters are, but I'll never again feel such unrelenting terror when I'm around them."

"I'm so proud of you, Niki." He held her close against his chest.

"Did you see how fast we went, Sundance and me? I thought maybe we should trot, but Travis said that's a harder gait to ride than a gallop so—"

"Niki, will you slow down? I want to—"

"Clay, I wasn't any worse than some of the other contestants." She grabbed his arms and stared up into his face eagerly. "Did you see the one from Houston? I don't think she'd ever been on a horse before. She was as scared as I was."

"I tried to tell you that you didn't have to be a cowgirl to be Queen of the Cowgirls. But that's not what I want to talk to you about now. If—"

"And I even turned loose of the saddle horn eventually!" Throwing back her head, she closed her eyes in an ecstasy of relief. "I can't tell you how relieved I am that—"

"Niki, dammit, shut up and let me tell you I love you!"

Her eyes flew open and her heart stopped beating. "You love me?"

"Of course I love you. Don't tell me you're surprised."

"But when I said I love you, you just yelled at me about trying to ride."

"I was too shocked to think straight. Now I'm not, and I'm saying I love you, and if you don't marry me I'll—I'll jump on old Sundance and carry you away. For real, this time."

"Oh, Clay, we can't do that." She collapsed back against his chest, her fingers digging into his shirtsleeves.

He nuzzled her hair. "I don't see why not."

"I can tell you why not. Because Dani would kill me if I let anyone else ride that horse." She smiled to herself. "So you can't carry me off, but maybe this time I'll carry you off."

"I'd love to see you try," he said just before he tilted her face up and kissed her as if he'd never let her go again.

AND SO IT CAME to be that all the competitions were finally over and nothing remained but to name the winner of the Queen of the Cowgirls title. Standing on the platform with the other contestants again, Niki dug fingernails into her palms to steady herself.

She hadn't enjoyed this competition, but she'd managed to survive it. She'd smiled and answered all the stupid questions put to her—"And how would *you* go about ending world hunger, Ms. Keene?"—and put on the stretch-denim swimsuit and the sequin-striped chambray evening gown without a murmur, pirouetted and smiled and smiled and pirouetted until she thought her face would crack or her knees buckle.

Now, resigned to the inevitable, she waited for the final axe to fall. At least she had Clay, she consoled herself—or would, just as soon as this was over.

At the microphone, Eve smiled like the Cheshire cat. Travis was also on the platform, although standing a little apart from contestants and officials. He looked grim. Niki hoped that didn't mean another bump in the rocky road of his romance.

"Ladies and gentlemen," Eve said into the microphone, "I want to thank all of you for coming, and all our contestants for taking part in our little contest. Remember, everyone on this stage is a winner today, not just the three lucky finalists. Each will be featured in her own ad for Mother Hubbard's Wild West Duds and will receive many other prizes."

Polite applause. Then: "Without further adieu, here are the three finalists. Please come forward when your name is called. Grace Stanley...Niki Keene...and Diana Dodd. Ladies and gentlemen, one of these women will be our new Queen of the Cow-girls."

Feeling the weight of an albatross around her neck, Niki smiled and waved with the others. Off to one side, she saw the pitying look on Clay's face. He finally seemed to understand how she felt, now that it was too late.

Eve spoke. "Our third runner-up is—*Diana Dodd!*"

The redhead stepped forward with a mechanical smile to accept a bouquet of long-stemmed roses. Blond Grace Stanley turned to Niki and grabbed her hands.

"Good luck," she burbled. "I hope I win but if I don't, I'm glad it's you!"

Niki didn't roll her eyes the way she wanted to. They'd never exchanged so much as a word, but what the heck. "I feel just the same way about you," she averred. "Good luck, Grace. Really, *really* good luck."

"Ohh..." Grace threw her arms around her only remaining competition in a bear hug.

"Isn't that sweet?" Eve said. "Such good sports. Let's put them out of their suspense, okay? The winner of the first Queen of the Cowgirls competition is..."

Niki braced herself.

"Grace Stanley!"

Shocked to the soles of her feet, Niki stumbled and nearly tumbled off the stage, saved from a nasty fall by Travis's quick reflexes. Through a haze of disbelief, she watched Clay move forward to present the thrilled winner with a new Stetson sporting a diamond hatband.

Which was all right until Grace threw her arms around Clay's neck and planted a big kiss on his mouth. His mouth might be on Grace's, but his gaze slanted to Niki, who could barely keep from laughing with hysterical relief.

Of course, she'd never lost a beauty contest before, so that was a bit unsettling but...

Travis spoke in her ear. "When this bedlam calms down, Eve and I want you and Clay to join us for a drink."

"Glad to."

And she was. They'd dodged a bullet! She didn't know how or why, but she was so very grateful.

Life was good! Hallelujah!

HOURS LATER, two couples sat on the manicured terrace of Eve's southern mansion, sipping mint juleps and watching the sun go down. No one had yet broached any subject of particular interest, all seeming content to simply come down off the roller coaster that had been the contest.

After a while, Eve said, "I hope you're not *too* disappointed, Niki dear."

"Not at all." But she was, just the tiniest little bit. She really wasn't used to being a good loser. Like everyone else in her hometown, she'd assumed that if she competed she would win. Then when Clay said the outcome had already been decided, she was *sure*.

Clay. She smiled at him, sitting next to her with her right hand gripped tightly in his left, as if he was afraid all this happiness would dissolve around him.

He leaned forward. "Which brings up another point, Eve. You made it very clear that if Niki competed, she'd win. What happened to change your mind?"

"Shh!" Eve raised her brows. "I wouldn't want her to think this contest wasn't on the up-and-up."

"Which it wasn't," Travis put in.

Eve pursed her lips. "You two! Okay, the truth is— Travis talked me out of it. He said if I put Niki through a year of hell, he'd—" She stopped speaking, her smile impish. "Let's not go into that. Suffice it to say that he blackmailed me and I succumbed."

"Travis!" Niki laughed at her benefactor. "Whatever you said or did, thank you."

"You're welcome." He looked like a cat who'd swallowed a canary.

"One more thing," Clay said. "What was that about using each contestant in an ad? First I'd heard of that."

"Oh, I've got a number of fabulous ideas," Eve said airily. "It'll take me a while to explain the new concept, but if you've got the time—"

"We don't." Gripping Niki's hand, Clay stood up abruptly. "Niki and I have things to do."

Eve laughed. "I'll bet I know what," she said. "All right, run along, children. Perhaps Travis will keep me from being *too* disappointed."

Niki hoped so but it wasn't the most important thing on her mind.

CLAY FUMBLED with her shirt buttons, his fingers made clumsy by eagerness. "I love you, Niki," he panted. "I love you more than I ever thought I could love anyone. I..." Her shirt fell away and he stared at her beautiful breasts, revealed by a sheer bra. "...never thought I could ever love anyone more than I love me, but I do."

"That's my test of true love, too." She shoved her hands up beneath his shirt to curve over his chest. "When you left the Bar-K, I thought it was all over, that you'd got as much as you could from me and didn't intend to waste anymore time."

He unbuckled her belt and pulled it free of the denim loops of her jeans. "You were an immovable object."

"But you were an irresistible force. It never occurred to me that I could actually do what I did— ride a horse and eat my words about competing. It was only when I thought your future was at stake that I realized—"

His hand beneath her bra made her catch her

breath. "Clay, we're so lucky it came out the way it did. Promise me you'll love me forever!"

"Forever and a day, starting now. Starting right now."

Picking her up, he carried her to the bed where he deposited her on the silky sheets of the honeymoon suite, then proceeded to make long, slow love to her.

He'd wanted a cowgirl and he had one, one he would keep.

Forever....

Epilogue

CHRISTMAS IN HARD KNOX was a joyous occasion that year for all the usual suspects, plus Eve Hubbard on the arm of her fiancé, Travis Burke. Tilly Collins, everybody's favorite Mrs. Santa Claus, sat on the dais next to Mr. Santa Claus in the form of Dobe Whittaker, beaming happily at the mob crowding into the community room.

She was especially delighted for her triplet granddaughters, their husbands, children and children to be. Dani and Jack had two, Petey and Elsie; Toni and Simon were expecting their first in February and looked happy enough to burst; and Niki and Clay...

Niki and Clay had flown to Las Vegas to marry right after that goofy contest—goofy in Tilly's eyes because her beautiful granddaughter hadn't won. Of course, if she had, it might have changed a few things Tilly would just as soon not mess with.

She sighed with pure satisfaction. Her granddaughters didn't really need her now. This was what she'd dreamed of when they left Montana to make a new life in Texas. Remembering the sign Dani had nailed to their door before they drove away—*Gone to Texas*—brought a smile to Tilly's lips.

They'd gone to Texas, all right—and found love. That was all she'd ever asked for them.

After losing her own daughter, Tilly had raised these girls to adulthood, worried about them and cared for them and loved them. Now her own time had finally come at the age of eighty-three. She waited with gleeful anticipation for Eve's announcement.

Eve caught Tilly's eye and the old lady nodded. Eve strode to the small stage with determined steps, Travis looking resigned to following her wherever she might go. Plucking the microphone off its stand, Eve addressed the crowd.

"May I have your attention, please? I have a few announcements..." When all attention was on her, she went on. "I may have lost a Queen of the Cowgirls," she said, looking directly at Niki, "but that's old news. What I found instead was—a new face to represent Mother Hubbard's Wild West Duds on a brand new ad and personal appearance campaign from one end of the county to the other."

Niki frowned and looked at Dani, who peered at Toni, who shrugged and looked back at Niki. No one looked at Grandma. It obviously didn't occur to any of the three that she'd know anything.

Eve continued. "I thought you all would like to be the first to meet this new personality who's going to become a household name and face from ocean to ocean and border to border. Ladies and gentlemen, here she is now, the one...the only...the new and improved *Mother Hubbard!"*

Turning to Tilly Collins, Eve flung wide her arm.

Tilly stepped forward bowing and beaming and relishing the shock on her darlings' faces. *They ain't seen nothin' yet,* she thought smugly.

Just wait until they found out that Dobe Whittaker would be traveling with her!

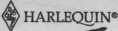

HARLEQUIN®
Temptation®

COMING NEXT MONTH